BLACK WIDOW

Borgo Press Books by S. Fowler Wright

Arresting Delia: An Inspector Cleveland Classic Crime Novel
The Attic Murder: An Inspector Combridge & Mr. Jellipot Classic Crime Novel
The Bell Street Murders: An Inspector Combridge & Mr. Jellipot Classic Crime Novel
Beyond the Rim: A Lost Race Fantasy
Black Widow: A Classic Crime Novel
The Capone Caper: Mr. Jellipot vs. the King of Crime: A Classic Crime Novel
Crime & Co.: An Inspector Cleveland Classic Crime Novel
Dawn: A Novel of Global Warming
Dead by Saturday: An Inspector Cleveland Classic Crime Novel
Dream; or, The Simian Maid: A Fantasy of Prehistory (Marguerite Cranleigh #1)
Elfwin: An Historical Novel of Anglo-Saxon Times
The End of the Mildew Gang: An Inspector Cauldron Classic Crime Novel (Mildew Gang #3)
Four Callers in Razor Street: An Inspector Combridge & Mr. Jellipot Classic Crime Novel
The Hanging of Constance Hillier: An Inspector Cleveland Classic Crime Novel
The Hidden Tribe: A Lost Race Fantasy
The Jordans Murder: An Inspector Combridge & Mr. Jellipot Classic Crime Novel
The King Against Anne Bickerton: A Classic Crime Novel
The Mildew Gang: An Inspector Cauldron Classic Crime Novel (Mildew Gang #1)
Murder in Bethnal Square: An Inspector Combridge & Mr. Jellipot Classic Crime Novel
The Police and the Public: Some Thoughts on the British System of Justice
Post-Mortem Evidence: An Inspector Combridge & Mr. Jellipot Classic Crime Novel
The Return of the Mildew Gang: An Inspector Cauldron Classic Crime Novel (Mildew Gang #2)
The Rissole Mystery: An Inspector Combridge & Mr. Jellipot Classic Crime Novel
The Screaming Lake: A Lost Race Fantasy
The Secret of the Screen: An Inspector Combridge & Mr. Jellipot Classic Crime Novel
Spiders' War: A Novel of the Far Future (Marguerite Cranleigh #3)
Three Witnesses: A Classic Crime Novel
Too Much for Mr. Jellipot: An Inspector Combridge & Mr. Jellipot Classic Crime Novel
The Vengeance of Gwa: A Fantasy of Prehistory (Marguerite Cranleigh #2)
Was Murder Done? A Classic Crime Novel
Who Murdered Reynard? A Classic Crime Novel
The Wills of Jane Kanwhistle: An Inspector Combridge & Mr. Jellipot Classic Crime Novel
With Cause Enough?: An Inspector Combridge & Mr. Jellipot Classic Crime Novel

BLACK WIDOW

A CLASSIC CRIME NOVEL

by

S. FOWLER WRIGHT

WRITING AS "SYDNEY FOWLER"

THE BORGO PRESS

An Imprint of Wildside Press LLC

MMIX

CONTENTS

CHAPTER I.

Chief Inspector Pinkey was annoyed. The crime (for he was disposed to agree with the view of the local police that the possibility of suicide could be eliminated) had been committed within a few minutes of 5:00 P.M. on Tuesday last, and now it was 11:30 on Tuesday morning; and it was only an hour ago that the assistance of Scotland Yard had been solicited by the Chief Constable of Buckfordshire, and within ten minutes of that telephone conversation he had been in a taxi for Paddington. Now he gazed at the high banks of the railway cutting, pleasant in October sunshine, as the train pulled slowly up the Chiltern gradients, and wondered how many clues had been blurred or obliterated before he had been called in to clear up a puzzle which the local officers had been unwilling to consider beyond their powers. Well, there was nothing new in that. He knew that it was of the first importance that he should stifle his annoyance and accept it cheerfully.

Any impatience on his part, any affectation of superiority, would make a difficult problem even harder than it must inevitably be. He must put aside all he had heard, all he had read, even all the possibilities that had engaged his mind as he had thought it over during the last few days (anticipating the possibility that he might soon be travelling in this direction), and approach it freshly. That was always the safest way. He got out at Ricksfield to change into the local train.

The village of Beacon's Cross lies about two miles from the station of that name. Inspector Pinkey remembered reading of this distance, and hoped that he would not be obliged to walk. Probably there would be a taxi. But you could never be sure at these little country stations. And he had a rather heavy bag. It was with a real gratitude, disposing him to unusual geniality, that he found himself being greeted by a tall man of somewhat military aspect, who announced that he was Superintendent Trackfield of the County Constabulary.

"I'm driving myself," he added, "so that we can talk freely. There aren't many places where you can be equally certain that you couldn't be overheard."

Inspector Pinkey had a moment of wonder as to whether this local policeman really believed this to be a remark of unusual profundity. Was he anxious to show that the country constabulary are shrewder than is commonly believed in the metropolitan area?

"Yes," he said, in a rather drier voice than he had meant it to be, "when you've looked under the seat."

"Under the seat?" Superintendent Trackfield had a moment of surprise. Then his face cleared. "Oh yes. I see. You don't mean that too literally. You mean when you've had a good look inside. Oh yes, of course."

By this time they were in the car.

The two officers exchanged platitudes upon the weather and the Cotswold Hills. Inspector Pinkey was too accustomed to the delicate operation of taking over investigations from less experienced or less competent hands to feel any awkwardness, but he knew the importance of doing it in a tactful way. It was to open the subject rather than to gain information that he remarked: "I understand that the inquest has been adjourned?"

But to Superintendent Trackfield, remembering the unadvertised reason for that adjournment, it was an unpleasant question to hear, and many would have given it a shorter answer. Chief Inspector Pinkey could observe that Trackfield might be obtuse, but he was an honest man. He said:

"Yes. You see, I told the coroner that we were about to arrest Lady Denton, and so he agreed to adjourn *sine die* in the usual way. After that Sir Henry said he'd like to go over the evidence again before we committed ourselves finally, and then he said he wasn't quite satisfied, and he'd decided to call you in."

Sir Henry Titterton was the Chief Constable of Buckfordshire.

"The evidence against Lady Denton must have appeared fairly strong. You felt satisfied of her guilt?"

The answer came rather stiffly. "Obviously. I applied for a warrant for her arrest."

Inspector Pinkey thought silently: "And you are still convinced of her guilt." He reminded himself again of the necessity of keeping an open mind. It might be true, as the obvious often is—but not always. What he said was: "Going by the Press photographs, she seems to be quite an attractive woman."

The Superintendent agreed. Exceptionally. He added that she was very popular also.

"Not the sort you would expect to be guilty of such a crime?"

"Not in the least." Trackfield was quite frank about that. The experienced ears of the Scotland Yard officer caught a tone which suggested that, though the speaker had been resolved to arrest her, he had not been entirely insensible of the lady's charm. It was confirmed by the remark that followed, rather stolidly spoken. "But you have to go on the evidence."

"That," Inspector Pinkey thought silently, "is an indisputable proposition, which makes it particularly important that the evidence should be considered by those who are most competent to handle it." But it was obviously not a reflection to be spoken aloud What he said was: "I was told—it was not in the press reports—that you are able to fix the time with certainty, owing to one of your own men having heard the shot."

Trackfield agreed again. "There is no doubt about that. But it was not one of my men. I was cycling along the lane below Bywater Grange when I heard the shot. I reached the station within five minutes, and it was then four minutes after five, as our records happen to show in a particularly conclusive way. Unfortunately, the exact time is not one of the decisive elements in the case. It does no more than confirm all the evidence of those who were in the house. Indeed, you may say that the time is the one point about which there has never been any doubt."

"Still, it's an advantage to know that we can accept that. I suppose you were quite near?"

"Yes, out of sight, but quite close. The lane is slightly hollowed, and there's a tall hedge. On the other side, a narrow strip of paddock divides the grounds of the Grange from the road. Sir Daniel's study faced that way, looking across a rather wide lawn to a strip of flower bed, and a background of laurels that hid the field fence from the house."

"And you heard or saw nothing beside the shot?"

"Nothing at all. Had I done so, I should have stopped to investigate then."

"Yes, of course. I suppose there was nothing remarkable in the sound of a shot coming from that direction? I dare say they'd often be potting a rabbit in the grounds?"

"No, I can't say that. I don't think Sir Daniel ever used a gun, or Mr. Gerard either. The gardener may take a shot at the birds sometimes, but I don't know." Inspector Trackfield had answered frankly, but he saw the implication of the question, which he did not like. He added: "It's just that there's so much shooting round here that we get in the habit of taking no notice. If I told our men to follow up every shot they hear, they'd be off the road half their time, and a nuisance to every neighbour I have."

"Yes, I see." The Inspector fell silent. He thought that, whatever absurdity there might be in ordering constables to investigate every shot they heard, it was a very different proposition that their Superintendent should ride on when he heard a shot in a house nearby, from which no sound should be expected to come, without investigating what it might mean. But it was a thought which should not be spoken aloud. He thought also that, if the tale told by the inmates of the house were true, there was no one (on his own account) who had been better placed than the Superintendent to have committed the crime himself. But it would be still more inexpedient to say that!

Still, he resolved to keep an open mind on that too. The fact that it was the Superintendent's own witness that he had heard the shot was in his favour, of course. But it might mean no more than that he thought he might have been observed as he rode away, and wished to disarm suspicion before it arose.

He looked at the Superintendent, and decided that it was not a probable guess. Still—he had proved more improbable things before now. Suppose that the Chief Constable had had the same idea, which was why he had refused the warrant for Lady Denton's arrest? Suppose he had hesitated to accuse his own assistant, and that that was why Scotland Yard had been called in? He must just investigate whether there had been any quarrel between the Superintendent and the dead man.

As he reflected thus, the car drew up at the police station and he went in to examine the statements which had been taken, on the particulars of which Lady Denton's arrest had been based.

He looked up from this perusal to ask: "Does she know I have been called in?"

"Yes. She has offered to put you up at the Grange while you are here."

"Then I may take that as arranged?"

"I said I would tell you when you arrived. I thought you might prefer to stay at the Station Inn."

"Any reason for that?"

"Only that you might feel freer to go about investigations in your own way. And if you're going to arrest a lady for murder...."

"Yes, I see. But I don't know that I am. We're all innocent, you know, till we're found out. You might tell someone to phone Lady Denton that I'll be there in an hour's time."

"There's one other thing—I don't say it's a reason why you should stay at the inn, but it's just a fact you might like to know before you decide. Redwin's still there."

"Redwin? I'm not sure I've heard his name yet. How does he come in?"

"Well, I can't say that he does. Only, he was the natural man to suspect. He'd been Sir Daniel's secretary for three years, and the only one he appeared to trust. And then he was suddenly accused of financial dishonesty, and turned out of the house. That was only a few days before Sir Daniel was shot. The tale is that there was a violent scene, and Redwin left protesting that he was an innocent man, and threatening that he'd make them sorry before he'd done.

"He wouldn't leave the district. He put up at the Station Inn, and went to Forbes and Fisher, a firm of Ricksfield solicitors who have a branch office here, and asked them to take up the case, which they wouldn't do.

"We've got two witnesses who heard him swear in the bar that he wouldn't leave till he'd had his rights, and that if he couldn't make Sir Daniel pay in one way, he'll find another that he'd like less.

"In fact, there was enough evidence against him to have justified detaining him on suspicion at once, but for one thing that there's no getting past—he wasn't there at the time."

"Certain?"

"Quite. There's the landlord himself, and two other witnesses—men who've lived here for forty years, and whose word anyone'd take. They don't love him overmuch either; but they'd all swear that he was playing billiards in the smoke room from four o'clock till after six, and we'd been called in, and Sir Daniel an hour dead, before then."

"That is if you can be sure that the shot you heard was the one that killed him."

Superintendent Trackfield did not look grateful for this suggestion. It was an idea which, until that moment, had not entered his mind, and, now that it was introduced, he thought that it approached the fantastic. His experience was that the obvious was most often true. He had passed Bywater Grange at 5:00 P.M. and heard a shot, where shots were not usually fired. It had afterwards been reported by various witnesses that a fatal shot had been fired at Sir Daniel Denton at the time in the library of that house. Obviously, the shot he had heard had been that from which Sir Daniel had died. It was equally obvious that those witnesses—six in all—could not all be wrong as to the time of the tragedy.

11

No; he hadn't considered that contingency, and he didn't blame himself in the least. He said: "I think when you've gone further into the case, you'll agree."

Inspector Pinkey, judging from the tone of this reply that he was on rather thin ice, became tactful again.

"Yes. I expect I shall. I don't think I'll go to the inn. The lady seems likely to be able to tell me more. You might let her know now. And when that's off our minds, perhaps you'll give me the whole story from your angle, and explain why you feel sufficiently confident of Lady Denton's guilt to justify locking her up."

"Yes, I can soon do that. The facts are simple enough, if we agree that Lady Denton must have fired the shot. It's only if we accept her story that they become hard to explain.

"Sir Daniel was in his study at the time. Lady Denton says that, as far as she knows, he was alone. The study has French windows opening on to the lawn. They were unbolted, if not actually standing wide. Sir Daniel's desk faces the window, and he appears to have been standing at it, having risen from his chair, but still facing the window, when the shot was fired.

"The door was behind his back. It opens on to a passage, which has the drawing room door almost opposite. Lady Denton says that she was in the drawing room when she heard the shot and the sound of Sir Daniel's fall—that was quite possible, he's a heavy man—and ran into the room. She says she saw him on the floor, bleeding from the head, and screamed for help.

"Sir Daniel's half-brother, Gerard, who lives with them, was in the library, the door of which is further along the passage. He says he didn't hear the shot or the fall—which is possible, too, for the library has a heavy, close-fitting door, and its windows are on the further side of the house—but he heard Lady Denton's scream, and ran to her.

"Lady Denton confirms this. She says he was with her almost at once.

"Mr. Gerard says that he went out on to the lawn to see if anyone was in sight. He cannot remember whether the windows were open, but, if not, they opened at a touch. He found the gardener's boy on the path, within sight of the window. He questioned him, and was told that no one had entered or left by that window for an hour or more previously, during which time the boy had been weeding the path.

"The head gardener was working at the side of the path somewhat further away, and out of sight of the window, owing to the curve of the drive. He is deaf and heard nothing.

"The boy says he heard the shot, and started to run to the window to see what it was, but the gardener called him back and told him to get on with his work.

"The gardener confirms this. He says that, being deaf, he heard nothing, but he was keeping a watchful eye on the boy, whom he charges with a habit of slipping round the house to talk with the kitchen maid more frequently than he approves. He agrees that the boy resumed his work when he called him back, and they both say it was not more than three or four minutes after that Mr. Gerard came out."

"Anyone else in the house?"

"No one except the servants. There are a cook, a house parlour maid, and the kitchen maid I mentioned before. They appear to have been about the kitchen or pantries at this time, within hearing and practically within sight of each other. Even if there were any reason to suspect any one of them of such a crime, they each have alibis from the other two. There was no one else in the house at the time."

"That is, so far as we know yet."

"Yes, of course. It didn't seem necessary to say that."

Inspector Pinkey realized that he had been tactless again. "Beg pardon," he said, "I didn't mean it the wrong way. I don't think I've often heard a statement so clearly put. What about the weapon?"

"It was a rather old-fashioned revolver which belonged to Sir Daniel, and which, if we're told the truth now, he used to keep very carelessly in an unlocked drawer of his desk."

"Lady Denton says that?"

"Yes. And Mr. Gerard."

"Well, they ought to know. No possible doubt that the bullet came from that gun?"

"Practically none. I ought to tell you that it's one of a pair, of which Mr. Gerard had the other. He told me about it quite frankly, and turned it up from the bottom of an old trunk. He said he hadn't fired it or had it out for years, which its appearance confirmed."

"How do we know that he didn't own both?"

"We've Lady Denton's statement as well as his."

"Yes, I see. Couldn't it have been possible for this Mr. Gerard to have run back to the library after firing the shot, and then come back when Lady Denton screamed?"

"We've her own evidence again against that. She says there wouldn't have been possible time. She says she went instantly when she heard the shot."

"Then it comes to this: that it was suicide, or she's shielding her half-brother-in-law, or else she did it herself, as you think she did."

"Yes, but she wouldn't shield him. I shouldn't say that they're on good enough terms for that. Not if she found she might be going to hang for him anyway."

"And, if you'd arrested her, it might have led up to the truth, even if she didn't do it herself? Well, I wouldn't say you were wrong, if you thought that—but what does she say herself? Doesn't she put forward any explanation at all?"

"She says he must have done it himself."

"And Sir Lionel Tipshift didn't agree?"

"No, we've got his report here."

"Yes, I've seen a copy of that, but it'll bear reading again."

Inspector Pinkey took up the report of the eminent Government expert, and read it as carefully as though he saw it for the first time. But he had finished it for some moments before he lifted his eyes from the paper and spoke again. He was silently reviewing the tale he had heard in a very experienced mind, and was inclining toward agreement with Superintendent Trackfield's conclusion. He thought it likely that Lady Denton's remaining hours of freedom would not be many. But he would see for himself, and resolutely keep an open mind until then. He mustn't even forget his theory that the Superintendent might have done it himself!

CHAPTER II.

Inspector Pinkey laid down the report. He had read that the bullet had entered under, and a little behind, the left ear, and had penetrated the brain in an upward and somewhat forward position. Sir Lionel Tipshift advised that it was possible—barely possible—for the wound to have been self-inflicted, if the weapon had been held in the right hand, passed under the left arm, and pointed upward. Possible—but absurd. He expressed a decided opinion that the shot had been fired by someone who had stood at the side of, but slightly behind, the murdered man. He thought it probable that this person had been considerably shorter than Sir Daniel. The muzzle of the weapon had not been less than two feet away from the spot where the bullet had entered. Probably rather more. Death must have been instantaneous.

"Was Sir Daniel," he asked, "a tall man?"

"Yes, unusually so. Lady Denton is rather the other way."

He knew that it was no more than he had expected to hear, and had to remind himself again of his resolution to remain unprejudiced until he had seen with his own eyes rather than through those of another man. Yet the inferences were obvious, and all pointed a single way. Someone known to Sir Daniel, who could approach him without suspicion. Who might stand beside him without causing him to turn. Who knew where the pistol was kept. Lady Denton fulfilled all these conditions. She might be the only one who would be admitted on that footing to her husband's study. And she was first on the scene, was there within a moment of the shot being fired, with only her own word of denial that she had not been there all the time. Yes, he was fair-minded enough to recognize that there had been justification for the decision to arrest her on the capital charge. But he would not say that as yet. He would see her first.

"There's one question," he said, "we haven't discussed yet. I mean motive. Motive isn't proof, and it's always dangerous to build on it alone. But it often saves a lot of trouble in pointing the right way for a second look. Anyone else round here with a grudge against the dead man?"

"It's not easy to answer that. He wasn't popular. There must be a score of neighbours who weren't sorry to hear the news. But there's a wide gap between that and a motive strong enough to lead to a crime of this kind. And there's some negative evidence on the other side. He doesn't seem to have been living any kind of a double life, nor even had any correspondence that he kept to himself. He was very careless about locking his drawers. He doesn't seem to have been blackmailed in any way. His wife can explain every payment his pass book shows."

"And negatively, as you say, that all seems to narrow it down to herself, even apart from the fact that you can't see how anyone else could have left the room without being seen by her or the boy. What about a motive for her?"

"It's much the same inside the house as out. He wasn't much loved, and I don't suppose anyone's really sorry he's dead. But the motives don't seem strong enough.

"As to Lady Denton, everyone knows he used to bully her, and, as a rule, she'd give way. Now and then she stood out, and they had a real row. They'd had one a few days before. She was quite frank about that. But on the whole they got on about as well as most couples do. He doesn't seem to have given her any occasion for jealousy, nor she him."

"What was the row about? Did she say that?"

"Yes. It illustrates the kind of man that he was. She says he went into the kitchen to countermand some instructions she had given, and said something that annoyed the cook, who appears to be the sort of woman who thinks the kitchen belongs to her. Anyway, she used her tongue at him, and he lost her temper with her, and in the end she told him to clear out of the kitchen, or she'd lay a broomstick across his back.

"After that, he told his wife to dismiss the woman, which isn't surprising; but for once Lady Denton stood up to him and declined. She told him that good cooks weren't easy to get, and he should leave the servants to her. They had a row over that, in which she got a bruised arm. She told me all this herself, and I had the cook's version as well. She doesn't profess to have much grief for his death, but she says, if he didn't shoot himself, she knows nothing about it, and can't suggest who did."

"Does she benefit by his death?"

"She gets control of some money which was in his hands before. Nothing beyond that."

"Is she in debt?"

"No. She tells me she has more money of her own than she has occasion to spend."

"How about the half-brother? Any motive there?"

"Yes, but again, it seems weak. Sir Daniel was sole executor under their father's will. He had control of funds which have been left for his brother's benefit, but so while he lived, he doled them out as he would. It is said that he used this power in vexatious ways, and Mr. Gerard must be very glad that it's ended now.

"But as a motive for murder—and one that appears to have been treacherously done, rather than in any excitement of quarrel—it seems a bit thin. And Gerald isn't the sort, to my mind, to take the risk of hanging without far more motive than that. He's too fond of his own comfort. He wouldn't risk being taken anywhere where he couldn't have breakfast in bed."

"Well, I expect you're right. You know the people, and I don't. But it comes to this—that you've discovered a certain amount of possible motive, and there may be more behind with one or other of them that we mayn't even guess yet. But I can see that I'm going to the right place. Which reminds me that, if I'm to be there within an hour of when you rang up, it must be about time to move. By the way, aren't there any finger marks on the gun?"

"Yes, Lady Denton's. There's an explanation of that, as she says she lifted it off the floor where it had fallen, and laid it on the desk. The constable who was called first confirms that it was lying there when he arrived. But if there are any marks besides hers, and one that's certainly Sir Daniel's, they're too blurred to recognize. So it's against her as far as it goes."

"Yes, rather heavily. There must have been ample time for her or the half-brother to wipe it clean, but she wouldn't wipe anyone else's marks off and then handle it again herself."

"No. If the murderer had escaped before she entered the room, he might have done so in theory, but that wouldn't have taken time, which, by her tale, he couldn't have had."

"So, unless it was suicide, it points straight to her."

Inspector Pinkey rose as he spoke, and was soon in the Superintendent's car again, on the way to Bywater Grange.

CHAPTER III.

Inspector Pinkey had shown already that he was a tactful man. He was given a fresh opportunity of demonstrating this when he was met by Mr. Gerard Denton with the news that Lady Denton had retired early, being unwell. Mr. Gerard was, perhaps, rather more apologetic than the occasion required. He alluded vaguely to yesterday's funeral. He said that Lady Denton had had rather a worrying time, which cannot be considered an over-emphatic description of the experience through which she had passed. He said that she hoped to meet the Inspector at breakfast on the following morning.

Having said this, he introduced his guest to a well-stocked library, and excused himself rather hastily, saying that dinner would be at seven-thirty. Inspector Pinkey decided that he was not eager to talk.

He had resolved to ask Lady Denton's permission before questioning the household staff, whether in or out. He had not anticipated that this would cause any delay, and it would be a courtesy which would cost him nothing, as it could not be refused. He now decided that another day would make no difference, in view of the time which had passed already, and he would leave everything (except, perhaps, Mr. Gerard) till the next day.

Gerard sat opposite to him at dinner, with Lady Denton's empty place at the table-head between them. The difference between brothers is sometimes very wide, and it is reasonable that that which separates half-brothers may be wider still. Sir Daniel had been a man of height and substance and an overbearing manner. Gerard was undersized, furtive, ingratiating. There is a type of woman who would have called him handsome, and he had the veneer of a gentleman.

He maintained a sufficient conversation on indifferent topics until Pauline, the pleasant, soft-voiced parlour maid who waited upon them, had withdrawn from the room; and then, somewhat to the Inspector's surprise, he brought up the subject of his brother's death, and discussed, with an apparent frankness, the problem which it presented.

He gave an account of his own experience which agreed substantially with that which the Inspector had heard already. He had been reading in the library and had not heard the shot, or, at least, not sufficiently distinctly to guess what it was. The doors of Bywater Grange were thick and well fitted. He doubted whether he would have been sufficiently disturbed or curious to enquire the cause, but that he had been roused the next moment by an agonized scream from Lady Denton—"Gerard! Gerard!"—and had run at once to her aid.

He told this tale clearly enough, though with some agitation of manner, and perhaps a little over-assertion, which might be natural under the circumstances. Supported as it was by Lady Denton's account, it seemed to remove suspicion from him, and concentrated it the more surely upon herself. He was evidently conscious of this, and showed some anxiety to assert her innocence. He dwelt on the note of surprise and horror which he had heard in her first scream. He admitted that he did not see how anyone could have escaped by the study door along the passage after the shot was fired without being seen either by her or him.

That being so, he inclined to the opinion that his brother had taken his own life. For what other explanation could there be?

He put forward the ingenious theory that Sir Daniel might have deliberately endeavoured to shoot himself in such a way that it would not appear to be his own act.

The Inspector agreed as to the possibility; but asked, why should he do that?

Gerard suggested spite against some individual (unspecified), or the household generally. No one who knew his brother would consider it an unlikely action.

The Inspector was not impressed by this argument. He could see no reason, at present, why Sir Daniel should commit suicide at all. But he observed that Gerard did not exhibit any regret at his brother's death, or anxiety that the murderer (if any) should be secured. If he were giving a true account, the evidence in his mind against his sister-in-law must be almost conclusively strong, for what was no more than unproved assertion to the Inspector must be certain knowledge to him. Yet it did not appear to have influenced him against her, whether because his appreciation of her character was sufficient to assert her innocence against any weight of adverse evidence, or that his feeling toward his brother were such that he did not care whether she had shot him or not.

The Inspector led the conversation in the direction of the ex-secretary, and learned that, in Gerard's opinion, there was little, if anything, too base or criminal for Mr. Redwin to attempt, no fate too dreadful to be deserved. It was evident that responsibility for Sir Daniel's death would be very gladly laid at his door. But he appeared to recognize, with whatever reluctance, that it would be difficult to establish the charge against a man who was playing billiards two miles away.

Dinner being over, Inspector Pinkey excused himself and went early to bed. He was a busy man, and accustomed to take sleep when he could get it. He had leisure to give some quiet consideration to Mr. Gerard Denton, who was of a type for which he had an instinctive antipathy, but he recognized that that was no evidence that he was responsible for Sir Daniel's end.

At present, on his own evidence, and that of Lady Denton, he was in an impregnable position; and this was supported by that of the gardener's boy, which eliminated the possibility that he might have left by the window, and returned to the library round the outside of the house. But could the Inspector accept this as final, and dismiss him from consideration? He was less inclined to do this owing to an idea which had come to him in explanation of the marks on the pistol, during the conversation at the police station, but which he had kept to his own mind. Suppose that Gerard Denton had used the weapon with a handkerchief or a gloved hand; or suppose, during the first moments of Lady Denton's agitation, that he had found an opportunity to wipe it, unseen by her; and had then suggested that it should be picked up, so that her finger marks should show upon it?

It was an improbable, but not impossible, explanation, and eliminated any question of the time necessary to clean it before the very hurried escape which he must have made.

It suggested that he was willing to throw the blame upon her, which his conversation did not confirm; but that might be no more than evidence of his own cunning. He might see that suspicion must ultimately settle upon her without any support from him, and the evidence that he would be prepared to give would be more damning if it seemed to come from reluctant lips. Or he might wish her no evil at all, providing only that there were enough suspicion against her to divert the lightning from his own head.

Ruminating over these possibilities, he was led to observe that it did not logically follow that, if Lady Denton had picked up the revolver, her brother-in-law had suggested the act; nor that, if it had been previously used in a covered hand, it was he who had worn the glove. He reminded himself of what an older officer had once said to him when he was busy with his first important case, and he had made report of various ingenious theories which he had constructed to explain a somewhat mysterious crime. "Son," he had said, "I can see you're a smart lad; but what I want to know is who killed Ben Jacobson, and one fact's worth a hundred theories for that."

One fact, as he had often observed since, was worth a hundred theories. And if facts should seem inconsistent or incomplete, the only remedy was to go on searching for more. So far, they all pointed one way.

But there remained the question of Gerard's character. That was not theory but fact, though it might be a fact which he did not completely know. Now he had seen the man, could he definitely eliminate him from the list of possible suspects?

He remembered Superintendent Trackfield's judgment that he was not a man who would risk his own life or liberty—and particularly not in a crime which must, if he committed it, have been deliberately and coldly planned—without a far more urgent motive than could be suggested against him.

"Well," he thought, "I should say that Trackfield was right about that." He even went further, to doubt whether any stress of difficulty would stimulate him to such a crime. He was rather, he thought, of the type of those who, in the extremity of disaster, will find courage to destroy themselves rather than to commit violence against those they may hate or fear. "And that," he thought, "would be his way out now, if he had done it, and thought discovery near."

All of which might be true, but it did not appear to approach the facts he already had. There was no evidence that Gerard had been threatened by any extremity of disaster, or had any reason to hate or fear his half-brother, adequate to stir him to the commission of such a crime.

"Well," he thought at last, "I must see Lady Denton. There may be no more in it than the reluctance which we frequently find among the local police of country districts to arrest those of good social position, unless they've got about ten times as much evidence as they'd think necessary to convict a shopman. I dare say, when I've talk to her for five minutes, I shan't need to look further away."

And with this thought in his mind he succumbed to the oblivion of a particularly comfortable bed.

CHAPTER IV.

Inspector Pinkey sat at breakfast with Lady Denton. They were alone. Mr. Gerard was understood to be having his breakfast in bed.

Lady Denton, after some preliminary courtesies, referred at once to the subject of her husband's death. "It is not," she said, "as you will suppose, a pleasant subject for me. It is one I would very gladly forget. But I understand why you are here, and if there's anything you would like to ask me, I hope you won't hesitate, whatever it is, if you think it might help to clear up the mystery."

"May I ask your own opinion, if you have formed one, Lady Denton?"

She paused before she replied, and then said: "I can't say that I've got one definitely. I didn't think he'd have done such a thing, and then I heard Sir Lionel's evidence that it wouldn't have been easy to do; and yet it seems the only solution."

She looked straightly at the Inspector as she said this. She had very beautiful eyes. She was a woman of fragile appearance, but with small firm lips and a rounded but resolute chin. Not one, he thought, who would have been bullied very easily, even by such as the dead man was said to have been. She added: "I know everyone's discussing whether I did it myself, and I half thought Inspector Trackfield meant to have me arrested before I heard you were coming. But you see, I happen to *know* that I didn't. So in that way I'm in a better position to judge than anyone else, and if I'm more inclined to think it was suicide, it may be a natural consequence."

Inspector Pinkey felt an awkwardness to which he was unaccustomed as his hostess expressed so plainly the suspicion which she knew to be directed upon her. He said: "Well, you see, in these cases we have to begin by suspecting everybody. You can't really blame him for that. There was one other question I thought I should like to ask you. Did you know—I mean, was it generally known that the revolver was kept in the desk drawer?"

"Yes, I knew that. Others may have done. I can't say for sure. I expect Mr. Redwin did, as he had charge of Sir Daniel's correspondence, and kept his drawers straight."

"Mr. Gerard?"

"Yes. I expect he would. You see, they both had revolvers of the same pattern, but of course you know that. I mean, he knew that Sir Daniel had it, but I can't say whether he knew where it was kept."

"Yes, so I had been told. Do you know whether Sir Daniel was in the habit of keeping it loaded? In an unlocked drawer?"

"I don't really know. I shouldn't have thought it was loaded. I don't think he'd have been so careless. He might leave any of his drawers unlocked. He was very careless about that."

"And there was a box of cartridges in the same drawer?"

"There was a box of something at the back of the drawer. I don't really know more than that. I never thought about it particularly. No doubt that's what it was."

Inspector Pinkey had an interval of silence. He gave some attention to his breakfast. It was really excellent bacon. He also considered the answers that he had just received. If they were true—and they appeared to be readily and frankly given—he could eliminate her from the enquiry. What remained? Suicide or Gerard Denton? Neither proposition could easily be reconciled with the facts as he knew them. He said: "In accepting a theory of suicide in a doubtful case such as this, it may be of great assistance if we can discover a motive—even one which may seem inadequate to a normal person. It is one of our difficulties that we can discover none here. Sir Daniel was in good health. We have the evidence of the post-mortem and of his own doctor, which you can probably confirm."

"Yes," she said, "he used to fuss over himself at times, but I never knew him really ill for a day."

"So I understand, and he appears to have had no financial troubles. Blackmail, or some other complication of double living, explains some cases, but we can learn of nothing of the kind here. His carelessness regarding keys, of which you have just told me, is consistent with the absence of such worries. I understand that his papers have disclosed nothing. His bank account has no unexplained debits. Only domestic unhappiness remains as a possible explanation of self-destruction. If you could tell me that there was such unhappiness, it might supply the motive for which we are seeking, though there would still be the difficulty of the shot coming from behind."

It was subtly if not unfairly put. She may or may not have seen that an affirmative answer might be held to inculpate herself as

23

much as it would support a theory of suicide, but she showed no sign of resentment, neither did she reply. She took up his last point only.

"Sir Lionel Tipshift considers it possible, as I have understood?"

"Yes, possible, and no more. But still, a motive of any kind...."

She was silent, and then said deliberately: "It is a matter which I would rather not discuss, even with you. Inspector Trackfield has led me already to say more than I meant or should. He is dead now, and if there was a little trouble between us at times—it was never much—I only wish to forget."

He recognized that she meant what she said, and that he could not press it further at that time. Indeed, her refusal to reply was admission enough. Not that he really believed in suicide. He thought it absurd. He said quickly: "How about his brother? Was he on good terms with him?"

"No, nobody was."

"You mean, no one was on good terms with your husband?"

"Yes, it wasn't easy."

"Well," he said, as Lady Denton rose from the table, "motive or no motive, it looks as though it's suicide that it's got to be. I may have to go back this afternoon. I'll just have a stroll round before I go."

"I've told the servants to give you any information they can, and to do anything you ask. I mayn't see you again if you're going back as soon as that." She shook hands with a slight but sufficient cordiality, and as she left the room, Gerard Denton came in, and when he saw Inspector Pinkey he did not look pleased.

He had come down in the complacent hope that he had allowed sufficient time for that infernal red-headed policeman to clear out. He couldn't think why Adelaide had allowed him to come to the house at all. Surely there were barracks for such as he! He tried with indifferent success at this second encounter to look the affability which he did not feel, but his ordeal was not prolonged. The Inspector had talked to him last night, and was not a man to waste words. Now he returned nervous civilities with others which were more self-confident, but equally insincere.

Then he went out, as he had told Lady Denton that he had intended to do.

CHAPTER V.

Inspector Pinkey, working upwards, which experience had taught him to be the more profitable direction in which to dredge for the gold of truth in the channels of muddles, errors, and lies beneath which he was accustomed to find it so deeply buried, commenced with the gardener's boy.

He was one slow of words, but of a perpetual grin. His lack of fluency was further impeded by the fact that, when Inspector Pinkey interviewed him, he was sucking a very large sweet. He said that he had heard the shot, and had commenced to run to the window in the anticipation—perhaps hope would not be an unfair word—that "somethin' was up." He had been called back by Mr. Bulger, and had reluctantly continued weeding until Mr. Gerard had appeared from the window and questioned him as to having seen anyone come out previously. Had he done so? No—no one. Except, of course, Mr. Gerard. How long after the shot was fired? Quite a time. Five minutes? Yes, perhaps. Perhaps not. Quite a time. Mr. Gerard had come straight to him to know whether he had seen anything. Then he had gone on to question Mr. Bulger.

This was the tale he had told before. There seemed no reason to doubt it, nor to hope that further questions would lead to any additional discovery.

The Inspector, determined that no possibility should be overlooked, found some difficulty in considering him as a candidate for the position of murderer. A boy's prank? Suppose he had discovered the weapon, so carelessly left in that unlocked drawer, during some lawless exploration of the vacant study?

Suppose he had hidden when Sir Daniel entered, and shot him from behind? He was short enough to have to fire upward at Sir Daniel's head. Suppose he had only meant to frighten him, firing up into the air? Suppose.... The Inspector reminded himself again of the relative importance of fact and theory; and these theories approached the absurd.

The character given to Sir Daniel did not suggest that his gardener's boy would be likely to play jokes with revolvers behind his ear. The Inspector looked at the cheerful, vacuous face, with its working jaws, as the sweet came back from the cheek in which it had been deposited for the exigencies of conversation, and the idea that he had deliberately shot Sir Daniel seemed too fantastic for further consideration. Still, if Lady Denton be put aside, he had been nearest to the scene of the tragedy. It was an explanation at least physically possible.

The Inspector's trained keenness of observation was inclined to perceive a suggestion of nervousness behind the obtuse screen of that perpetual grin. He knew that the country man or woman, with an appearance of slow stupidity, can often conceal thought or emotion far more successfully than his less stolid brother of the town. The boy had a reputation for slipping away from his work. He must have his own ideas, his own dreams of evil or good, through the long slow hours in which he pulled weeds from the garden path.

"Now, Tommy," he said, "tell me this. Did you run round to the kitchen, or go away for anything else just for a few minutes, so that anyone could have gone in at the study window, or gone out, without you seeing him, when Sir Daniel was shot? If you did that you needn't be afraid that you'll be blamed by Bulger or anyone else if you tell the truth, and you may save a lot of trouble all round."

The boy looked at him for a few seconds before replying, and the Inspector had an uneasy doubt that he was considering the expediency rather than the truth of the admission that he had been invited to make.

It would be of little assistance to the solution of the problem if the boy should make a false statement that he had left the drive, under the impression that he would be pleasing those in authority, or from whom his employment came.

But the Inspector was spared the embarrassment of that doubt, for, after his pause of silence, the boy shook his head in denial.

"How," he asked, "could I 'a' done that, with Mr. Bulger a-lookin' on all the time? You can arst him, if you like." And then, with a burst of convincing logic: "How could I 'a' heard the bang, if I warn't here?"

Inspector Pinkey recognized his defeat, and strolled on to interview the gardener, a rheumatic ancient, who received him in the steaming heat of the cucumber house, and appeared quite willing to converse on any subject, comparatively indifferent to the fact that his deafness frequently resulted in his remarks having little relation to those which were addressed to him.

However, by tact and patience, the Inspector finally obtained, in addition to some information respecting the domestic habits of cucumbers, and Mr. Bulger's opinion of Hitler (which was not high), the information he sought.

It appeared that the gardener had been trimming the sides of the drive, working toward the house, and therefore in Tommy's direction. He had kept a vigilant eye upon him, having too many previous experiences of his errant temperament to be careless in that respect.

His deafness did not prevent him from perceiving very quickly the implication of the Inspector's curiosity, which he appeared to regard as of a highly humorous complexion. He chuckled long over the idea of Tommy venturing into the study to make an end of his employer. "You be the fair limit, you Lunnon chaps," he said, in appreciation of so good a jest, and long afterwards, when the somewhat discomfited Inspector had endeavoured to lead the conversation in other directions, he broke into a new cackle of laughter, and remarked as though confidentially to the cucumber he was tending: "They be the limit, they be."

The Inspector left at last, having obtained Mr. Bulger's opinion (for what it was worth) that, if Tommy had succeeded in leaving his post, his objective would have been the kitchen, not the study, and that his desire had not been for his employer's conversation, but for that of Mabel, the kitchen maid, who was, to Tommy at least, a more attractive member of the community. But Mr. Bulger was emphatic that he had gone nowhere at all. The only time that he had shown symptoms of flight, Mr. Bulger had called him back, and that occasion had been shortly followed by Mr. Gerard's appearance, and was evidently that on which his curiosity had been roused by the sound of the fatal shot.

Mr. Bulger also expressed a decided opinion (which the Inspector was to find general throughout the domestic staff) that Sir Daniel had shot himself, in doing which he had shown a sound idea of his own value. Mr. Bulger pointed out that this was one of the points in which man was superior to the animal, and still more to the vegetable kingdom, there being fruit trees of indifferent bearing which Lady Denton was unwilling to condemn to the axe, of which there was too little hope that they would make an end of themselves in the same way.

The Inspector was also informed, in the course of a long metaphor of considerable complexity but unmistakable meaning, that it is meritorious to stir the soil either for the insertion of a seed potato or the removal of the resulting crop, but that the disturbance of dirt when you have nothing useful to sow, or profitable to reap, may be a less pardonable activity.

It was a reflection which came at times to his own mind, as it must come to all but the most obtuse of those who minister to the blind and cruel impartiality of the law. He was aware of the conventional, and perhaps sufficient, reply; but he knew that it is difficult to state it briefly in convincing words, and—to a deaf man—he let the case go by default, and walked round to the kitchen to see what, if anything, might be learned there.

It is no mean tribute to his tact and adroitness that he was able to overcome the latent hostility with which his investigation was regarded—doubtless in their mistress's interest—by the domestic staff. By these qualities patiently exercised, he was able to obtain a willing repetition of tales which had been fully told more than once before, and it was no one's fault that they did no more than confirm the narrative and conclusions which he had had from Superintendent Trackfield on the previous day.

If the servants had any doubt of how Sir Daniel had died, it was evident that it was one that they were not disposed to develop, even in their own minds; nor was their loyalty to their mistress shaken thereby. Sir Daniel, their answers assumed, if they did not assert, had died by his own hand, and if the cook did not actually add "and a good thing too," it was evident that she would have assented willingly to that proposition. Yet the Inspector had no difficulty in eliminating her as an alternative to the supposition of Lady Denton's guilt. Had Sir Daniel been banged on the head with a flat iron in one of the back passages, it might have been a more doubtful matter.

He gained nothing by these enquiries beyond the elimination of the indoor staff from the meagre list of those on whom suspicion might reasonably rest. His acquired habit of observation caused him to be more than subconsciously aware that Mabel, like Tommy, seemed to be fond of sweets of an unusual size, one of which, like him, she had found some difficulty in disposing of while she talked; but he failed (for which he blamed himself some hours afterwards) to see that there might be any connection between this coincidence and the cause of Sir Daniel's death.

He judged the results of the morning's investigations to be of an entirely negative character; yet the implicit championship of Lady Denton which he had encountered among the retainers of Bywater Grange, both inside and out, must have had some effect on his mind, for he found himself much less willing to return to headquarters with a report which would confirm the issuing of the warrant for Lady

Denton's arrest than he had been when he had parted from her two or three hours before.

He did not see how an interview with Sir Daniel's late secretary could alter the position in any way, in view of the excellent alibi which he possessed, nor what further enquiries could be made usefully in any other direction. The case seemed to be one to be placed before a jury, and which they must decide. Yet he resolved, even while he was listening to the cook's somewhat voluble opinion of her late employer, that he would not return without giving Mr. Redwin an opportunity of explaining the threats he had been heard to make.

He asked the parlour maid to tell her mistress that he proposed to trespass on the hospitality of the house for another night, but that he might not be in till late, and took a pleasant two-mile walk to the Station Inn.

CHAPTER VI.

It was a warm walk under the midday sun, and Inspector Pinkey entered the empty dining room of the Station Inn with a slight sense of fatigue, sufficient to double the comfort of the armchair into which he sank, and with an appetite which considered that lunch, due to be served in twenty minutes, could not arrive too soon.

But though his body relaxed in the cushioned ease of the chair, his mind was alert and active, and he was quickly and quietly aware of the entrance of another guest a few moments after himself, who sat down in such a position that he was out of sight unless the Inspector should turn deliberately round to survey him, which he was little likely to do, being satisfied that he could introduce himself better over the table of the coming lunch, if he should think it advisable to do so.

Nor was the newcomer so entirely beyond observation as he may have supposed, for there was a fire screen in the summer emptiness of the grate—a glass flower-painted screen, which reflected with sufficient clearness to inform the Inspector that he was himself being surveyed with more than the polite and casual interest that a fellow guest might be expected to show.

A few minutes later, when the waiter had entered with a steaming calf's head, and other dishes worthy of a larger assembly, Inspector Pinkey seated himself opposite to a man of something less than middle age, neatly dressed, and with an appearance of competence and self-possession. He had sleek hair, short and black, and dark eyes in a sallow long-nosed face, and the Inspector, expert though he was in such questions of identification, had some doubt of whether he might be the man he sought.

But it was a doubt that he need not show. He resolved to reveal himself, and, if it were not Redwin, he could turn the conversation so that no harm would be done.

He asked casually for a mustard pot that he did not need, and then added, in his less official manner: "Pinkey's my name, but I don't suppose you've heard of me before. I'd better give you a card."

He handed one over the table, which Mr. Redwin (for it was he) glanced at without surprise.

"So I supposed," he said sourly. "Something about Denton, no doubt? What do you want to know?"

There was a directness of approach here which could only be met in the same way.

"I hoped you might be able to give us information which would throw some light on the tragedy."

"Why me?"

"Because I understood that you were his confidential secretary until less than a fortnight ago."

"Then I suppose you heard how I left?"

"I have heard that you left abruptly, but I know nothing of the circumstances, nor am I particularly concerned to enquire. I am merely asking you to give assistance, which is the duty of every citizen under such circumstances."

Mr. Redwin made no answer to this. He went on with his meal as though he had not heard. The Inspector felt that it might be polite to add: "I need scarcely say that there is no suggestion that you had any complicity in the matter. If I ask your help, I am not therefore suggesting—"

Mr. Redwin interrupted him abruptly: "No, you couldn't." It seemed for a moment that he proposed to terminate the conversation with that curt interjection; but he went on: "Though it's no thanks to you that I'm not in jail now. Do you think I don't know how everyone's been badgered to say they're not sure I was here? If I'd happened to have been out walking that afternoon, you'd have moved all heaven and hell to find some pretext to run me in."

There was a tone of mingled anger and contempt in this speech which made it evident that there would be no willing help from Mr. Redwin unless he could be brought to a different mood.

The Inspector was not in the habit of making outside reflections upon the local police whom he might be called in to assist, but he felt that the position justified him in remarking: "I'm sorry if anything's been allowed to happen which you have good ground to resent. I only came down yesterday afternoon."

"Well, it wasn't any too soon." The words were ungracious, but the tone was somewhat friendlier than before, and encouraged the Inspector to a further approach: "It must have been a shock to you when you heard of his death?"

"I couldn't say I was over surprised."

31

"Do you mean you had any reason to expect such an event?"

"No, I wouldn't say that. But I might have made the right guess."

"Do you mean you had reason to think that he'd shoot himself after you'd gone?"

"No, why should he?"

"You don't think it was suicide?"

"No, I don't."

"Do you mean you had reason to suspect that he might be murdered?"

Mr. Redwin seemed about to reply, and then pulled himself up, as though wondering whether he might be saying too much.

"Inspector," he said, after a time, "you're asking me a good many questions. Do you mind if I ask you one for a change?"

"Not at all. Of course, I can't promise to answer till I've heard what it is."

"Well, that's how I feel about yours. But what I'd like to know is whether there's any law against slandering people to the police, because if so I'd rather not say any more. I've had trouble enough."

"If you've any honest suspicion that you can't prove, you can tell it to me in full confidence that I shall not let it go further until it's been properly verified and confirmed. And if you've got such a suspicion, I need scarcely say that it's your duty to speak."

"Well, I suppose that's what you'd be expected to say. But I'm not so sure. They might say it was malice, coming from me, and I don't know where it might end. A man can have thoughts that he doesn't speak. Not that I ever heard, anyway. I think I'll just sit back and watch how the game goes."

Inspector Pinkey controlled a natural irritation to say quietly: "I don't think we can leave it there, Mr. Redwin. It seems to me that you've said too little, or else too much.

"I've told you that I'm sorry if you've been annoyed by any enquiries that the police felt it their duty to make, but you must see, if you look at it fairly, that you brought it more or less on yourself. Unless people are saying things about you now that are not true, you had made threats in public places against Sir Daniel that brought suspicion on you inevitably when he was found shot as he was.

"I've told you that we're not accusing you, as we know you were here at the time, but if things stand as they do now when the inquest's resumed, there may be evidence that these threats were made, and there'll be a vague suspicion against yourself that you'll find it hard to shake off. I suppose you know how people talk, without troubling to get the facts straight. And if that kind of talk once begins, it gets worse as the years go on.

"It seems to me that you've got more interest than most in getting it properly cleared up, and the truth proved, whatever it may turn out to be."

Mr. Redwin listened to this argument with an expressionless face. Then a slight smile of derision came to his lips as he asked: "And you want to make me believe that you can't see through it without my help? Well, you may be right about that. But I don't know—"

The sentence stopped abruptly as a bucolic couple, delayed at the local cattle market, noisily and hastily entered the room.

The Inspector cursed inwardly, and then considered that there might be no loss on either side if there should be an interval for reflection on that which had been said already.

He rose and called for his bill.

"Well," he said, with as much geniality as he felt able to show, "you might think it over, and we'll have another chat later."

He held out a hand, which was somewhat reluctantly taken, and went out to face the two-mile walk back to the police station. He felt that he would be glad of the quiet opportunity of reviewing a suggestive and yet rather baffling conversation. And after that he would have another talk with Trackfield. He saw that he was not likely to go back tomorrow. There was more in this than appeared. It was unfortunate that he could form no opinion as to what it might be.

CHAPTER VII.

"I've been trying to get in touch with you since before lunch," Superintendent Trackfield began, as Inspector Pinkey entered his office, and before he could commence the narrative of his own experiences. "I had Forbes and Fisher on the phone just before noon. They wanted to know when the adjourned inquest would be likely to be held, or if there were any other developments in connection with Sir Daniel's death. They seemed to want to know more than they liked to ask, and when I told them that you were down here, and had the case in hand, they were anxious to speak to you, if possible, before three o'clock, when they have an appointment with another solicitor, who's arriving here from London on the two-fifty."

"Any idea what it's about?"

"I asked that, of course. I told them that we should be more likely to be able to help them if we knew why the information was required. They were very guarded in their reply, but I gathered that it is some financial question regarding Sir Daniel's estate. I didn't press it beyond that, as I felt the matter was in your hands. I rang up Bywater Grange, and learned that you were staying there over tonight, but that they weren't expecting you back until late, so I thought you'd be likely to look in here before long. I promised Fisher I'd ring him up again at two-thirty, and let him know if I'd been able to get in touch with you."

"What did you say the name of the firm is?"

"Forbes and Fisher. They're the leading firm in these parts. It's a branch office here."

"Didn't you mention them once before?"

"Did I? Oh yes. It was they whom Redwin asked to take up his case, and they turned him down."

"But he surely wouldn't have gone to Sir Daniel's firm? He couldn't have been his secretary for three years without knowing who his lawyers were."

"They didn't act for Sir Daniel, as far as I've heard. His lawyers were a London firm—Scarf, Scarf, and Wheeler. I don't know how Forbes and Fisher come on the scene now."

"Well, we soon shall. And if they want information from us, I think I'll invite them to say what Redwin asked them to do for him, and why they refused."

"You don't think he was concerned in Sir Daniel's death?"

"No, I don't. But I've had lunch with him, and I've seldom met anything more suggestive than the things he hints, and won't say. I haven't done with him yet."

"He must have seen a good deal, living in the house for three years. But we've got to remember that he's a malicious and discredited man."

"There's no doubt he's malicious. As to being discredited, I should say we ought to reserve opinion till we know more about how he came to leave the house in that sudden way. I shall be interested to hear Lady Denton's account of that."

"You haven't got anything specific from him so far?"

"No. He wasn't easy to handle at first, and the conversation was broken off when some men came into the room. He professed to be very bitter about the enquiries concerning his own movements which you very properly made. I told him that he brought them on himself, and he'd always be under some vague suspicion unless the matter were properly cleared. I can't say he opened up after that. But he made it plain that he thought it was murder, and that he wasn't surprised—that was the significant point—that it should have happened soon after he left. He hinted that if we were any good, we should be able to manage without his help."

"Well, perhaps we shall. You haven't been down here for twenty-four hours yet, and things are beginning to stir."

It was a generous speech, as Inspector Pinkey could not fail to perceive. The Superintendent might still wonder in his own mind whether it might not have been as well to arrest Adelaide Denton at once, as he had decided to do, and how things might have gone then.

But he knew that whatever development there might now be would be ascribed—perhaps justly—to the superior technique and wider experience of the Metropolitan officer. Only in one event—if he should ultimately come to the same conclusion as to Lady Denton's guilt—would Superintendent Trackfield be confirmed in the Chief Constable's eyes as being adequate to the office he held. He did not exactly desire her conviction. She was an attractive lady, against whom he would have said that such an accusation was absurd a short fortnight ago. But he would not have been normally intelligent—and he was something better than that—had he not seen the position in which he stood.

Inspector Pinkey was moved to reply with equal generosity, and partial truth: "You mustn't thank me too much for that. I've done no more at the Grange than to confirm what you'd done before. And whatever these lawyers are going to spill, you'd have got without help from me. I shouldn't wonder if I'm back in London in a couple of days with no more to report than that you were taking the right course when you decided to give the lady a rent-free lodging."

"Well, it still points to her. If we could get something more in the way of motive than we have now...."

"Yes—if, as you say. We may be coming to something we haven't guessed, and we can't tell where it'll point. But it's about time we gave these gentlemen a ring up."

A moment later the Inspector was informed that Mr. Fisher's voice was at the other end of the wire.

"Yes," he said. "Inspector Pinkey from Scotland Yard."

"Could you tell me if the adjourned inquest on Sir Daniel Denton is likely to be held at an early date?"

"I am afraid I can't give you any information unless I know why it's required."

"It is in connection with an important point which has arisen in the course of the realization of Sir Daniel's estate."

"Realization? Isn't it rather early for that? I shouldn't have thought you'd have had time even to prove the will."

"Well, perhaps it wasn't quite the right word. I should explain that we are not the solicitors for Sir Daniel's estate. We are acting for other interests. The question of proving the will does not arise."

"Can't you be rather more definite?"

There was a moment of silence before Mr. Fisher replied, with a note of hesitation in his voice: "I'm afraid not, not on the telephone, anyway. Would it be too much, Inspector, if I ask if you could give me a call?"

"No, I'll do that. When would you like it to be?"

"At once, if you can. I should like to see you before—well, straightway, if you can."

The Inspector turned from the instrument to ask: "How far off are they? They want to see me now. Can I get a car?" The heat of the afternoon was increasing, and he felt he had walked enough.

Being reassured on these points, he replied that he could be with Mr. Fisher in five minutes, and hung up the receiver.

CHAPTER VIII.

Mr. Fisher was a small, precise man, with little indication of age or youth, except in the greying of his close-cropped hair. He had a formal and somewhat hesitant manner, springing rather from habitual caution in the choice and use of words than any lack of confidence in his own capacity.

"I must thank you, Inspector Pinkey," he began, "for your courtesy in calling upon me at such short notice, and on so vague a pretext. I am expecting several gentlemen here in about twenty minutes, and I shall be glad to give you a short explanation before they arrive of the business which calls them here, and, I hope, receive such information from you as will simplify the position."

"Are you asking me to meet these gentlemen?"

"That must be for you to decide. I hope it may not be necessary."

"Well, I expect you're right. We'd better not decide that till I understand what the trouble is. I need scarcely say that I shall be glad to give you any help I can consistently with my own duty. In fact," he added, "I was going to ask a somewhat similar favour from you.

"There's a man named Redwin hanging about here who used to be Sir Daniel's secretary (by the way, I wonder what he wanted a secretary for?), and was kicked out, so it is said, a few days before the death occurred. I'm rather anxious to learn anything I can about that."

Mr. Fisher hesitated. He glanced at the clock. It was evident that he was unwilling to be diverted from that which was on his own mind. But it was a difficult request to rebuff, in view of that which he had to make.

"I need scarcely say," he replied, "that I shall be glad to give you any help that I can. I believe Mr. Redwin actually came to see us. He would have seen our Mr. Weedon—our managing clerk at this branch. I do not know much of what passed, but I can tell you definitely that we are not acting for him."

"So I was told. Perhaps if I could have five minutes with Mr. Weedon? We should still have time for a talk before the other gentlemen are due to arrive."

Mr. Fisher hesitated again. He looked once more at the moving hand of the clock, which was now at two forty-five. "If you will excuse me a moment," he said, "I will ascertain whether he is here now."

Having said this, he did not ring for the information, though there was an office telephone on his desk, but went out of the room. The Inspector judged that the probability that he would be introduced to Mr. Weedon before the coming interview was not great.

He was left alone for about three minutes, when Mr. Fisher returned alone.

"Weedon," he said, "is engaged with a client, but I have had a few words with him. We will do all we can, of course, but your request places us in a rather difficult position. My view, with which I hope you will agree, is that if certain information is communicated to us with a request that we will act professionally upon it, such information is confidential, even though we may decline the business. It is confidential up to the moment when we decline to act, and remains so up to that point."

"And there it naturally ends?"

"That is a reasonable presumption." He paused, and added with an impressive deliberation: "Mr. Redwin, after having been told that we were not prepared to act for him, made the gratuitous remark that we could please ourselves, but she'd be sorry before he'd done."

"She?"

"Yes."

"Meaning Lady Denton, of course?"

"It is a natural deduction, which I am not prepared to dispute."

"I may conclude that he had some plan of blackmailing her, with which a firm of your reputation naturally declined to be mixed up?"

"That must be your own conclusion. It is not a question to which I am in a position to give a negative reply." He added, as though fearing that he had said too much: "Blackmail is, of course, a particularly vague word. I am not sure that a legal definition exists. If I may offer a word of probably quite needless advice, I would suggest that anything coming from that source should not be lightly believed. I am told that he has been heard—outside this office—to express a strong animosity against Lady Denton, and I should suppose that he is a clever and unscrupulous man."

He glanced at the clock again, which was now at six minutes to three. "Will you permit me now," he asked with a slight smile, "to put another matter before you?" The Inspector was not clear that he had gained much, though it might be another pointer on the right road, and, in any case, as much as Mr. Fisher could fairly give. He felt that he could no longer delay to listen to the business which brought him there.

"Yes," he said, "it was kind of you to let me in first." And as he settled himself to listen, a clerk came in with a strip of paper which Mr. Fisher read, and then said: "Ask Mr. Strange to wait a few minutes; and Mr. Wheeler, and Mr. Borman, if they get here before I ring."

He commenced at once, as the clerk went out, speaking rather more rapidly than his habit was, though still with some deliberate precision.

"I must be brief, and come to the point by a shorter road than I meant to take. There is a question arisen in an acute form regarding a certain clause in an insurance policy under which Sir Daniel Denton's life was covered for a large amount. It is a matter which immediately concerns the local branch of the London and Northern Bank, whose manager is waiting to see me now. Mr. Borman, the solicitor to the bank (whose country agents we are), is on the way here, and I have asked Mr. Wheeler, Sir Daniel's own solicitor, to be present also, as I suppose he will be acting for Lady Denton, whose interests may be at stake."

"I suppose the question is whether he committed suicide?"

"Yes, in the first place—yes."

"And that implies that his life was insured for some large amount within twelve months of his death?"

"Yes, but there is an explanation of that. Of course, the verdict of a coroner's jury is final on such a point. We understand that the inquest is now adjourned *sine die*. If you could assure me that it is likely to be held within fourteen days—"

"I'm afraid I couldn't do that. But I think I can go as far as to say that, on Sir Lionel Tipshift's evidence, it's unlikely—extremely unlikely—that any jury could return a suicide verdict. I should say that the policy will be almost certainly paid."

"I was inclined to anticipate that reply. Unfortunately, that conclusion only raises a further question of a more delicate kind. There is a rumour that reached the bank yesterday—I am not at liberty to say how, but you know how important it is that a bank should be fully informed, and how numerous their sources of information are—a rumour which is probably quite baseless, and which I should not mention but that it is unavoidable, that there was a suspicion that Sir Daniel had died by his wife's hands—that, in fact, a warrant had been already issued for her arrest."

"I can tell you definitely that that is untrue."

"I am pleased to hear it. I have met Lady Denton socially, and the rumour appeared incredible. Can you tell me that it is a quite baseless report?"

"I don't know that I ought to say more than I now have. You will appreciate that I have not been on this case for more than twenty-four hours. At the present moment there is no accusation against Lady Denton of any kind. May I say that, if you eliminate the possibility of suicide, as I think you may, it is difficult to understand how it can be a question of such urgency, or how it can affect the validity of a policy on Sir Daniel's life?"

"I have not said that it would. But the legal position is somewhat complicated, and counsel's opinion was being taken upon it in London this morning, the result of which I have not yet heard. You are doubtless aware of the principle that a man cannot profit from his own crime?"

"Yes, I see."

As Inspector Pinkey said this, he rose up to go. He held out a hand which Mr. Fisher delayed to take. "If you would like to remain....," he said tentatively.

It was the Inspector's turn to hesitate. If he resolved to stay, he might hear things which it would be very useful to know. But he could not discuss the case at this stage with the various gentlemen who were about to assemble there.

"I should be pleased," he said, "to remain, if it be understood that I shall not be asked to say more than I have already done."

"Very well, I will ask them in. I have no doubt that they are waiting now."

A minute later the three gentlemen entered the room.

CHAPTER IX.

The bank manager, Mr. Strange, was a man of middle age, slightly bald, slightly rotund, with a reputation for few words, and a placidity which remained outwardly unruffled by this unexpected disturbance in the smooth working of the largest account but one on the books of the branch he ruled.

Mr. Borman, the acting head of a firm of solicitors who specialized in the higher ranges of banking law, and who drew an income therefrom about equal to that of three High Court judges, was a tall, well-groomed man with a natural air of dignified authority, and a cultivated suavity which was liable to turn to sarcastic curtness if his sense of logic were tried too far, or his dignity took offence.

The other lawyer, Mr. Wheeler, was of a different type. He recruited clients on the golf course, or in the ten-shilling enclosure, who were handed over subsequently to the ministrations of his more industrious partners. He had a wide knowledge of men, and a sufficient knowledge of law. His usual joviality was now subdued to a wary reticence. Naturally of a more robustly combative temperament than were, perhaps, any of the four other gentlemen who were round him now, he had come prepared to express his mind with any necessary emphasis on behalf of a dead client, and one who lived.

But it was not for him to begin. He had not called the meeting, for which he would have said that there was no reason at all. He came to listen, before he could have occasion to talk, and he had been careful to join the train at the last moment, travelling in a different compartment from that which was dignified by Mr. Borman's occupation, and to order a vehicle in advance to meet his arrival, so that they should not be invited to enter a single taxi.

"I think, Mr. Fisher," Mr. Borman observed, "now that we are all together, if you would give us a short statement of the position, particularly for Mr. Wheeler's benefit, it might be a convenient course to adopt. Unless, of course, you have obtained information

41

since you phoned me this morning, of such a definite character that it is needless for us to pursue the subject at all."

"I'm afraid," Mr. Fisher replied, "I cannot go quite that far. We have the benefit of the presence here of Chief Inspector Pinkey, of Scotland Yard, and he is prepared to tell us that the medical evidence is strongly opposed to the theory of suicide, and that the report which has unfortunately reached us regarding Mr. Wheeler's client is without foundation. He does not wish to discuss the matter further at this moment, having only taken it up during the last twenty-four hours, but perhaps you may consider that that is all which we need, or are entitled to know."

"I would prefer, if I may," the Inspector said, "to put it in my own words. The result of the post-mortem is such that, apart from any new evidence, which we do not anticipate, it is improbable that any jury would return a verdict of suicide—in fact, it would be an act of perversity on their part to do so.

"I am told that you have heard a report that a warrant has been issued for Lady Denton's arrest, which I think it my duty to contradict, as it is untrue."

Mr. Borman said: "Thank you, Inspector. That is quite clear. May I ask whether the date of the adjourned inquest has now been fixed?"

"No, it has not."

"Do you anticipate that it will be held at an early date?"

"I am sorry that I cannot answer that question."

Mr. Borman looked at Mr. Wheeler and the bank manager, rather requiring than asking their assent, as he gave his judgment on these replies: "Then I am afraid we are much where we were before. I'm afraid we must go on."

"Gentlemen," Mr. Wheeler interposed, "I think I ought to say one word before you begin. I have come to listen, which I am prepared to do, but it must not therefore be understood that I consider that there was any proper occasion to ask me here.

"I heard of this suicide suggestion from you before, and I told you, from my knowledge of Sir Daniel's character, you needn't give it another thought. I now hear, for the first time, that you've been entertaining another rumour of a grossly slanderous kind, and we've all heard that it's as false as you might have guessed it to be. I don't say that this isn't a privileged occasion, and I won't ask you where it began, but if I catch anyone repeating it outside this room, they'll have a writ just as quickly as we can get it issued."

"Perhaps, Mr. Wheeler," Mr. Borman suggested, with an air of suave authority which approached rebuke, "if you would kindly hear

Mr. Fisher's statement first, so that we should be clear as to what we have to discuss—"

"Well, I've said I'll do that. But I should like to point out first that the obligations of the bank are under a deed which is not impeached by my client's death, and of which the covenants on our side have been fully performed."

Mr. Borman did not offer any comment on this. He gave a slight sign to Mr. Fisher, who understood that the conversation was not to be continued on their side. He commenced his statement accordingly:

"Sir Daniel Denton, as we are all aware, has been engaged during the last few years in financial transactions of a somewhat extensive and decidedly speculative character, the means for which have been largely supplied by an overdraft, for which he arranged by the deposit of certain securities with the local branch of the London and Northern Bank.

"Somewhat less than a year ago, he required not only additional accommodation at the time, but the assurance that some large sums would be contingently available at later dates. He had acquired a very large block of Medwin-Badcock shares, which were only partly paid up, and on which a further call, involving an immediate payment of thirty thousand pounds, was liable to be made at any time after the end of September of this year, and this call has, in fact, been made, and the money is now due.

"Sir Daniel at that time had a large income—far beyond his expenditure—derived from the life interest in his mother's Edgley estate, which, in the absence of more direct heirs, now passes absolutely to his cousin, Benjamin Sidmouth.

"In purchasing these shares, Sir Daniel very naturally wished to be assured in advance that, if such a call should be made, he would have the necessary funds available for its satisfaction, and he therefore entered into an arrangement with Mr. Strange by which this money would be found, if and when it might be required, against a charge of five thousand pounds per annum upon the life interest I have mentioned.

"But as that interest would cease—as, in fact, it has ceased—at his death, the bank very properly stipulated that they should have the additional security of an insurance upon his life for the full sum of thirty thousand pounds; for which purpose certain existing policies for smaller amounts were cancelled, and a single new one was issued for that sum. I am afraid that these details, which it is necessary to recite, can be of little interest to you, Inspector. If you have given us all the help you can, and would wish to withdraw—"

"If you are reciting them for my benefit," Mr. Wheeler interposed, in a tone less rude than the words suggested, "you are really wasting your breath, for I am already conversant with Sir Daniel's affairs."

"Not at all," Inspector Pinkey answered the previous speaker, "if I have your permission to stay. You are giving me information which I am glad to have. Do I understand rightly that Sir Daniel's death was of no financial benefit to—to any members of his family?"

Mr. Wheeler took the answer upon himself. "Yes, you certainly may. Very much the reverse. The larger part of his income ceased with his death."

Mr. Fisher did not approve the vicarious answering of a question which was addressed to himself. He ignored the interruption, and was precise in reply.

"I believe that, under the terms of Sir Daniel's will (for probate of which I understand that Mr. Wheeler has already applied), Lady Denton is his sole heir. But, as you have heard, the major part of his income has ended with his decease. So far as Mr. Gerard is concerned, an income which Sir Daniel was administering for his benefit now passes into his own control. There is no change beyond that."

"There is no suggestion," the Inspector continued, "that Sir Daniel was financially embarrassed by his speculations? I should like to know whether he may have left a substantial estate, apart from the life interest which has now ceased."

The first question was answered by two voices at once.

"No," Mr. Fisher replied, in a coldly judicial manner, "I should say not."

"You may take it," Mr. Wheeler said, with more emphasis, "that he was not embarrassed at all. His investments were very soundly made."

The second query caused Mr. Borman to break the impatient silence with which he had listened to this disorderly interruption of the business which brought him there.

"That," he said dryly, "is what I understand we had come here to decide."

Inspector Pinkey had the wisdom to become silent. He realized that the less his presence was emphasized, the more he was likely to learn. He had an instinctive perception that Mr. Wheeler was annoyed at his being there, and he was prepared to withdraw at once if any protest should be made. Mr. Wheeler's feelings were just what he supposed them to be. Considering that the question of whether

Adelaide Denton had murdered her husband could never be far below the surface of the discussion which was before them, it was
natural that her solicitor should consider that few men could be less
appropriately present than the Scotland Yard officer who had the
official investigation in hand.

But he considered also that the harm, if any, had now been
done. It might be increased if any protest should come from him.
Beyond that, he saw that the Inspector wished to remain, and he was
too shrewdly aware of how much human prides and weaknesses enter into these matters to wish to antagonize him in any way.

He had been conscious for some days of the peril of Lady
Denton's position. He had resolved, only a few minutes ago, that
when that meeting was over he must not return to town without a
call at Bywater Grange. He must form his own opinion of her guilt
or innocence, must induce her to confide, if possible, in himself; and
if it should appear that it was her own hand that had fired the shot,
he must consider how suspicion could still be stifled, or how best he
could contrive a line of defence which would bring her free. He realized that he might soon be meeting the Inspector again, though he
did not know how very soon it would be.

Meanwhile, the fact of the Inspector's presence was causing
him to take a more emphatic tone than he might have thought necessary had he been dealing with his fellow lawyers alone. In his own
mind, he recognized the awkward position in which the bank was
placed. But Mr. Borman was quite capable of protecting that institu-
tion without help from him. His duty was to watch Lady Denton's
interest, and assert her rights.

Mr. Borman, having led the meeting back to the business which
brought them there, came to the point at once.

"The fact is, Mr. Wheeler," he said, "I can't advise the bank to
find such a sum as thirty thousand pounds, unless there is a reasonable certainty that the insurance money will be paid; and, as Lady
Denton's interests as Sir Daniel's heir are so deeply involved, I
thought it no more than courteous to yourself to let you know how
the case stands."

"I don't want to be rude," Mr. Wheeler replied "but I don't see
what option the bank has got. We're not negotiating now. It's a matter of reading the deed, and you'll find there couldn't be anything
much clearer than that."

"I may tell you," Mr. Borman replied, in more temperate words
than those which Mr. Wheeler employed, but with a formal aloofness of manner which tipped the scale to the other side, "that we
have taken counsel's opinion upon the points involved in our deci-

sion this morning, and it is upon that opinion that we are proceeding now."

"Then what," Mr. Wheeler asked abruptly, "are you proposing to do?"

"Unless substantial further security can be put forward, we have no option but to dispose of the shares. Even now, apart from the insurance policy, it appears that we are not fully secured."

"You mean, you'd knock the bottom out of the market by throwing all those shares on it, just as a call's being made, and sell them for half what they're worth, and then point to the wretched price you got to justify what you'd done."

"I mean that a security's worth no more to a bank than it will fetch at a forced sale. I don't need to tell you that."

"No. And the question doesn't arise. You've got no right to sell; and I don't see what I can do beyond sending you a formal protest, and a warning of the responsibility you incur."

"I am sorry you take it in that way. We had hoped that there might be other assets available with which to support the account. I suggest that it could be no loss to your client, under any circumstances, to take that course; unless you set up the position that the estate is insolvent, or think it preferable that the shares should be sold."

Mr. Wheeler declined to discuss these propositions, seeing to where they might lead.

"You can't ask me to do that," he said. "The will isn't even proved. You'll find you'll get the insurance money all right in the end. You're going head on for an action for damages that'll hurt you a lot more than paying the call, and all for no real reason at all."

"I'm afraid it's a risk we must take," Mr. Borman replied, in a tone that suggested that there would be no sleep lost over that decision. He added, in his suave manner: "I don't want you to think that we're inclined to act harshly in this matter. I think you should know that we've been in communication with the company's solicitors already, and that we had arranged for some delay in paying the call, without formal default, if we could give a near and definite date on which the matter would finally be dealt with. You will appreciate that that was not a simple matter to arrange, with so large an amount involved."

"I wouldn't be too sure about that. I don't suppose they want all those shares thrown on the market just now."

"But," Mr. Borman went on, ignoring this interruption, "it now appears that such a date cannot be given. I am afraid you must take it as definite that I cannot advise a course which might finally leave these shares on the bank's hands. You must remember that, when this call is paid, there may be others to follow in future years. The bank does not normally care for securities of that nature."

Mr. Wheeler repressed an inclination to retort: "Oh, don't they? What about their own shares?" But he had been thinking quickly while these exchanges were made, and what he did utter was the laconic query: "Fifty-fifty?"

Mr. Borman, experienced and adroit in his own way in such negotiations, had yet some difficulty in avoiding expressions of bewilderment and then surprise.

"Do you mean," he asked, "that you might be prepared to support the account with an additional fifteen thousand pounds, if we should accept that as sufficient?"

"Well, I don't say but I might. There's some money of Lady Denton's that's not earning much now. And there'd be no risk that I see. It would have to be quite clear that there's no bargain about the deed. The deed stands. It's entirely a question of what interest it will save. It's got to be an investment proposition, and nothing else."

"I don't think," Mr. Strange said, speaking for the first time, "that there need be any difficulty about that."

Mr. Wheeler rose to go without further words. He said briefly to Mr. Borman, who now shook hands in his most affable manner: "If you tell your office to get in touch with our Mr. Spencer in the morning, any time after ten-forty-five." Then he said genially to Inspector Pinkey, who also had risen to go: "Coming my way?" To which that gentleman gave a ready assent, without asking what it might be.

They walked out together, leaving the very capable representatives of the London and Northern Bank satisfied that they had found a better issue out of a worrying position than they had expected to reach.

Mr. Wheeler was also well content. He knew that Adelaide Denton's money would not be jeopardized unless the insurance policy were finally declared invalid, and possibly not even then. He was convinced that suicide could not be established. Only if she were accused and convicted of her husband's murder.... What he had done was to throw her money into the scale as a demonstration of the absurdity of the idea. And how could it be used, in her interest, for a better purpose than that?

CHAPTER X.

Inspector Pinkey, following in the direction that Mr. Wheeler led, and exchanging the preliminary platitudes about the vagaries of English weather, with which those who are of slight or recent acquaintance habitually prelude any serious conversation, observed that they were heading for Bywater Grange.

"I expect," he said, in cautious approach to the subject that was on both their minds, "you will be seeing Lady Denton while you are here?"

"Yes, I am going there now. I shouldn't wonder if I have to ask her to put me up for the night. There are several matters of business that I may as well clear up while I am here."

The Inspector, seeing that Mr. Wheeler appeared to have come down with no more of the necessities of individual comfort than his pockets might be supposed to hold, concluded silently that the intention of staying must have been formed since he had heard the suggestion that his client might be in danger of arrest on a capital charge.

"If you do that," he said, "I may see you again. Lady Denton has kindly offered me the hospitality of the Grange."

If Mr. Wheeler felt any surprise at this news, he gave no sign. He said: "Excellent...I need scarcely say that if Lady Denton or I can give you any information or help, you have only to let us know."

"Yes, Lady Denton assured me of that."

The Inspector spoke with more reserve than before. He did not intend that this genial solicitor should take charge of himself, or the case that he had in hand.

Mr. Wheeler, very sensitive to atmosphere, perceived that he must move cautiously here.

"It is most desirable," he said with gravity, "in Lady Denton's interest, that the murderer should be found."

"Yes, I should say that it is."

Mr. Wheeler reminded himself that he had not yet seen Lady Denton, and that it might be wiser not to develop conversation with the detective till he was better informed of what might have passed already between them. He became silent, and felt some relief when the Inspector paused at a branching road, and said: "I'd better not come further with you now. I told Lady Denton I shouldn't be in till late. I expect I shall see you at breakfast, and perhaps we can have a chat then."

"Glad to, if you're not too late down. I shall have to leave in time to catch the nine twenty-four."

"Oh, that's all right. Breakfast's never too early for me."

They parted with some recovered cordiality, born of the fact that they were both getting what the moment required, which was to be alone with their own thoughts.

Mr. Wheeler walked on to the Grange, revolving a speculation which had crossed his mind during the discussion of the suicide theory that afternoon. He had dismissed it with a word of contempt, and he still thought it a most improbable thing. But suppose that Sir Daniel had had that clause of the insurance in mind? Suppose he had tried to shoot himself in such a way that it would appear certain that he had been shot by another hand? He did not think it probable, for he could see no reason why he should want to shoot himself at all, and, in any case, it was not an idea to be spoken aloud, with £30,000 to be lost if he could make it believed.

Only—if it were agreed that murder had been done—if the insurance money were paid—if Lady Denton (it was a possibility which he saw that he ought to face) should be put on trial after that—then, and not till then, such a theory might be advanced, to confuse the minds of a jury who would surely be reluctant to convict an attractive woman of such a crime—a stupid, improbable, almost incredibly motiveless crime, as it must appear to be.

He saw the weaker side of the case, if the theory of suicide should be pushed aside. The unanswered question—who was it, if not she?—but he felt some confidence in his case—he was always confident in himself—that even if Adelaide Denton should be arrested on such a charge, he would be able to bring her off. He felt some confidence in his client also, that she would not fail in nerve or courage, and of her appearance—that vital weapon in the defence of peccant women—there could be little left to desire.

He wondered also what might be the activities of Chief Inspector Pinkey: where had he been going, and with what object now? Perhaps he was already on the actual culprit's track, and Lady Denton might be in no danger at all? But, curiously and illogically enough, though he had formed an opinion that the Inspector was a man for his friends to trust and his foes to fear, and though he was resolved not to consider even the possibility of Lady Denton's guilt, he had no real expectation that any energy of detection would produce a man who had fired the shot. Perhaps the absence of any theory of motive behind the crime, of any guess of whom the murderer would be likely to be, assisted to give a feeling of unreality to the pursuit of that theoretic criminal. He was not a living man, to feel the handcuffs on his wrists and to be lodged in a prison cell, but rather one to be postulated for the defence of a woman who might stand in the dock, where it was difficult to imagine that he would himself appear.

With such thoughts in his mind, he went on to Bywater Grange, to be warmly welcomed by Lady Denton, who felt a natural relief in the presence of one whom she recognized as both a loyal friend and a powerful ally. Her only equal confidant having been Gerard Denton during the stresses of the past week, it was a pleasant contrast to talk to one of so absolute a contrast, both in brains and courage.

He had come down, he said vaguely, to meet the bank's solicitors in reference to some matter concerning Sir Daniel's estate, and it was not until he was seated on her right side at dinner, with Gerard Denton opposite, that he led up to the subject on which he felt there must be something more to be said, by remarking that he had met Chief Inspector Pinkey at Forbes and Fisher's—"a very capable officer, I should suppose him to be."

"Yes," Lady Denton replied; "he is staying here. I expect you heard that?"

"So he told me. I must try to get a chat with him before I leave. I hope to ascertain what progress he has been able to make, if the official reticence can be overcome. There are business reasons why it is important to clear up the circumstances as promptly as possible."

Lady Denton did not avoid the issue, nor did she shrink from plainer words than he had thought it tactful to use. Her eyes met his as she asked: "You mean the circumstances of my husband's death?"

"Yes. It is particularly important that the question of suicide should be eliminated."

"But that's what I think it was."

"I'm afraid the medical evidence makes it difficult, if not impossible, to adopt such a conclusion. Incidentally, if that view were accepted, it might involve a loss of thirty thousand pounds to your husband's estate."

"How could it do that?"

"There is an insurance policy for that amount which would be invalidated if Sir Daniel took his own life."

Lady Denton was silenced for a moment by this information. She looked down in a frowning thoughtfulness, but when she spoke she held stubbornly to the opinion she had expressed before.

"Well, I told Inspector Pinkey I thought it was that. I don't see how it could have been anything else."

"Did he appear to agree?"

"He didn't say anything."

"I only asked you because I heard him say this afternoon that we could put the idea of suicide out of our minds. He is sure that Sir Daniel died by another hand. I wished to know whether he were being as frank with you as I am sure that you were with him."

"He didn't say much. He just asked. I told him I wished I could help him more, but I didn't see how I could."

"If you just tell the truth," Mr. Wheeler replied, watching her with a friendly keenness while he spoke, "you don't need to worry beyond that. It's almost always the best way."

"It's the only way here," she said in a definite tone, which should have reassured, but left him vaguely dissatisfied.

Mr. Gerard Denton had listened to this discussion with the expression of one reluctantly present at a conversation of unpleasantly indecent character, which he is unable to stop. Now that it paused, he said irritably: "I can't think why you ever let him enter the house."

"Inspector Pinkey? Perhaps it's because I'm not quite a fool."

Her tone was sharp as she addressed her brother-in-law, but she was smiling as she turned to Mr. Wheeler in explanation. "Gerard always did object to men with red hair."

Mr. Wheeler appeared uninterested in this curious antipathy. He said: "I think you took a wise course."

"It seemed sense," she replied. "Gerard won't see that it's the best thing that could happen that someone with brains and imagination should take it up. Superintendent Trackfield couldn't get beyond the fact that I was first on the scene. I believe he'd have accused me of shooting Daniel myself, if it hadn't been too absurd."

Mr. Wheeler did not feel able to reject that possibility, remembering what he had heard during the afternoon. "I suppose," he said, "that the police's difficulty is to explain how anyone else could have been there. But doesn't the idea that no one left by the window after he was shot rest entirely on the evidence of the gardener's boy?"

"Yes. He was weeding the drive."

"I should like a few words with that boy before I go back to-morrow."

"You'll get nothing out of him," Gerard interposed sulkily. "He's too dense."

Lady Denton confirmed this, though in a different tone. "If he doesn't take to you, you'll do all the talking, and he'll just grin."

Mr. Wheeler was left in some uncertainty concerning her attitude. She appeared indifferent. But he was sure that Gerard would prefer that he should not question the boy, which he became more resolved to do.

He left that subject to ask: "I suppose Redwin's still hanging round?"

"Yes, he was till yesterday anyway. He's put up at the Station Inn."

"I suppose you can't connect him with it in anyway?"

"No. They say he was playing billiards all afternoon." She smiled slightly as she added: "I believe the police were quite annoyed about that."

"Yes, I expect they were. But I wish you'd tell me just how he left, and why. I know that Sir Daniel turned him out of the house on an accusation of dishonesty of some kind, and that he was vowing vengeance against you both; but I never heard the details of what occurred. In fact, I never saw Sir Daniel alive after I had a brief note from him to say that I was not to pass Redwin's signature in future on any document without reference to him."

"Of course I'll tell you," she replied, "if you're really anxious to know, but does it matter now?"

He saw that she was reluctant to speak, but he felt that, for her own sake, he must have whatever information Inspector Pinkey might be obtaining in other ways.

"Yes," he said, "I think it does. A man may be responsible for that which he does not do with his own hand. The question of an accomplice cannot be dismissed without more knowledge than I have now. Besides, Inspector Pinkey will be interviewing him. There can be no doubt about that. And I should like to have some idea of what tale he will be likely to tell."

He thought there was some effort of self-control behind the smiling lightness of her reply. "You can be sure of one thing. There'll be nothing good about me." And he noticed that she made no further demur about giving him her account of the events which had led to Mr. Redwin's abrupt departure from Bywater Grange.

"I don't really know," she said, "what he'd done wrong, or how much. I just told Daniel about a matter that seemed queer to me, and I found I'd put a match to something that blew up with a bang.

"It was a letter to him from Mr. Strange at the bank, which was in the same envelope as one to myself about my own account. I suppose that was a clerk's mistake, but it turned out that whatever Mr. Redwin had been doing had been quite open, and the bank had no idea that Sit Daniel didn't know everything. Mr. Redwin is a very clever man, and I suppose he thought it was quite safe, and, if anything *were* found out, it would look best for him.

"You see, Sir Daniel had got to trust him entirely. He used to open all the correspondence, and keep all the business accounts.

"It was about two years ago that Sir Daniel was associated with some men who were trying to get control of the Catstein Syndicate, and I knew that Mr. Redwin was helping him then to buy in other names besides his own. Then there was a quarrel, and the thing dropped.

"A few weeks ago I noticed a report that the Catstein shares were going up, and when I mentioned that to Daniel, he said it was nothing to him. I remember the expression he used, that he'd sold out every damned share he'd got twelve months ago. So when I saw this letter addressed to Mr. Redwin about a dividend cheque for a rather large amount on Catstein Syndicate shares, I remarked about it quite casually when we were all at lunch together.

"Mr. Redwin said they were a little side speculation of his own, and I suppose, if that were true, there'd have been nothing wrong; but Sir Daniel wouldn't leave it at that. He went into all the figures himself, and said he found that he had bought a thousand shares more than he'd been paid for, and that Mr. Redwin had falsified the amount to make it square on the books.

"Of course, Mr. Redwin didn't admit that. He gave some explanation that I didn't understand, and they were at it in the study for an hour or more after.

"Then they came in here together. Sir Daniel said: 'Adelaide, I've given Redwin half an hour to pack up. If he doesn't want to be thrown through the window, he'll be out of the door before then.' Mr. Redwin was just as angry, but in a quieter way. He said: 'You'll think better of this by tomorrow.' And he added something about some papers that Mr. Thompson might be interested to see."

"Who is Mr. Thompson?"

"I think he meant the Income Tax Inspector. That's his name, anyway. But Daniel got more angry than before when he said that. He said: 'You just try it on, and I'll see that you get five years, if you get a day. You ought to be glad enough to get away with a whole skin.' And after that Mr. Redwin went upstairs to pack."

"Well," Mr. Wheeler commented, at the end of this narrative, "that's clear enough, and very much what I thought. But if that's all there is in it, I don't see why he should have his knife into you."

"He thought I did it on purpose to get him out of the house. You see, we had never been friends. He wasn't the sort of man I could like, and I didn't want Daniel to have a secretary at all. I didn't want him to speculate as he did. There was no need, for we'd both got more money than we ever spent; and he wasn't easy to live with if he thought things were going wrong."

The tale was, as Mr. Wheeler said, very much what he had expected to hear, but he would have been glad if there had been more. For there was nothing in this to suggest an explanation of Sir Daniel's violent end, whether by his own hand, or that of another man. And he saw that Redwin's alibi was of an impregnable strength.

Yet here was a man shot, and another with whom he had quarrelled a few days before, and who, after he had been rebuffed in an attempt to secure legal redress, had remained in the neighbourhood, threatening the vengeance which he still hoped to inflict. There seemed an almost overwhelming probability that there must be some connection between the two, and, if there were, it appeared to him, on the partial knowledge that he then had, that it must be very greatly to Lady Denton's advantage to lay it bare.

"Well," he said, "if that's all you know, we must hope that Pinkey'll find out a lot more."

Lady Denton did not respond to this suggestion, but she rose from the table a moment later with the remark that she would be glad if he would have coffee with her in her own room. The words were said in a way that put her half-brother aside, a position which he accepted without demur, going out by another door.

CHAPTER XI.

Lady Denton sipped her coffee, and gazed into a fire which had been necessitated by a chilly October evening, following the warmth of a sunny day.

Her companion, seated on the other side of the little coffee table, was as silent as she. He knew that she had not brought him there to chat of indifferent things, and he thought it best to wait her own time to begin.

"What I told you," she said at last, "was quite true."

"So I supposed."

"But it was not everything."

Mr. Wheeler did not look surprised at this statement. He may have had a slight doubt as to whether he were going to hear all the truth now. Had that long silence been occupied in deciding how small a further instalment might serve her need? Or had she even been considering whether she would be secure from detection in a useful lie? With all his experience he could not be sure. But she was his client, and till the contrary should be proved, he must accept her statements as the instructions on which he was bound to act. Unless, of course, he must resist or refuse them for her own good.

"It is always difficult," he said, "in a matter of this kind, not to leave something out. It's sometimes hard even to judge which may be the really important things."

"Yes," she said, in the tone of one who might be in such a doubt as she spoke. And then: "I don't think Daniel was really glad that I found Mr. Redwin out. I think he'd suspected before, but hadn't wanted to see. He wasn't easy to get on with at times."

"Meaning Sir Daniel?"

"Yes."

"So," he said, "I had understood."

He was patient, understanding that these were little more than meaningless words, while she hardened her resolution for that which she had to say.

"You knew Mrs. Caver," she said at last, "my sister, who died last year?"

"Yes, we acted for her in the divorce."

"Yes, I remembered that. She came to stay with me for a week when she first quarrelled with John. That was a year before."

"I don't think I knew that; but it was a very natural thing to do. How does that matter to us now?"

"She had some of Percy Hudson's letters with her then. I tried to persuade her to burn them, but she wouldn't do that. She was afraid to take them with her when she went back. (They made it up at that time.) She said John would find them. In the end, she left them with me, to be taken care of till she asked for them again."

"And how does that matter now?"

"Mr. Redwin took them when he went up to pack. At least, I suppose it was then."

"You needn't trouble about that. After the divorce, and your sister's death—"

"Mr. Redwin thought they were written to me."

"Do you mean that he tried, or is trying, to blackmail you about them?"

"He told me that he would send them to Daniel unless I got him to take him back."

"Which you very properly refused to do?"

"No, I tried, but Daniel wouldn't listen. I didn't suppose he would."

"But if the letters were not for you, I don't see why you should care."

"Daniel mightn't have believed that."

"But the name would have proved it."

"They weren't—I mean, such letters often aren't written so that you can be sure. It might be just a pet name. Something silly. You know they are, more often than not."

"Then there'd be no proof that they were written to you more than to anyone else."

Lady Denton seemed to puzzle over this for a moment, as though it were a fact that she had overlooked, and was now unprepared to meet. Then she said: "But he must have known the envelope they were in. They were in a large envelope that had been addressed to me before I used it to put them away."

"Who must have known?"

"Sir Daniel, of course. You keep asking questions, and I'm not telling it the right way. When I went to him, I saw the envelope on his desk."

"You mean when he was shot?"

"Yes."

"Where is it now?"

"I burned it the first chance I got."

"I should doubt the wisdom of that. Had anyone seen it beside yourself?"

"No. No one could, except Gerard, and he wouldn't have noticed it. Not then. I saw it as he went out at the window to see if the man who shot Daniel was still there. I burned it—all the letters, I mean, just as they were, in the grate here that night."

"What do you suggest that this had to do with Sir Daniel's death?"

"I don't know. I suppose nothing at all. But I thought that you ought to know. If Mr. Redwin gets talking to the Inspector, I don't know what he might say."

"Nor do I, but you can be sure there's one thing he won't do. He won't mention those letters. He won't accuse himself of such conduct as that. Not unless he's quite mad."

Lady Denton accepted this assurance with an expression of some relief, though she may have observed with a natural annoyance that if that judgment were sound, there had been no occasion to expose the incident, even to Mr. Wheeler's professionally friendly ears. Certainly she would not have told it, but for an uneasy doubt of what story Mr. Redwin might have prepared for the Inspector's consumption.

"Well, I'm glad I know," Mr. Wheeler said, "and I'm not sure but it might be worse. I shouldn't lose much sleep over that. But I'll get up in the morning in time to have a good talk with Inspector Pinkey before I go. By the way, was the drawer open or shut? I mean the one from which Sir Daniel, or someone else, must have taken the pistol before he was shot."

Lady Denton seemed somewhat confused by the abruptness of this question. "The drawer?" she said. "Oh, open. No, I mean shut. Yes. I'm quite sure about that."

"And you've really told me everything now?" Mr. Wheeler asked this in a casual, reassuring tone, as though everything were not much. But he looked keenly and somewhat anxiously at his attractive client, for how could he fight her battles, if she kept back half the truth, as he knew that some women will till they are driven back to the last ditch, or even a fatal minute longer than that.

"Yes," she said, "I've told you everything now. And, so far as I'm concerned, I think it's enough too."

CHAPTER XII.

When Inspector Pinkey parted from Lady Denton's, solicitor, he did not return to the police station, nor did he descend again upon Mr. Redwin to resume conversation with him. He turned into a quiet lane, the stony surface of which offered some guarantee against the noise and nuisance of motor traffic which it is now so hard to escape within the confines of any civilized land. He felt that he needed an opportunity of reviewing the knowledge which he had gained during the day, and he knew from past experience that he could do this best while taking the quiet exercise of a country walk.

He did not suppose that all, if any, of the new facts he had learnt would be of any assistance in solving the problem with which he dealt. The interactions of life are too complex and too inconsequent for that. He would be fortunate if none of them should lead him astray.

But, so far as they might appear even remotely relevant, they must be patiently considered, both in themselves and in relation to others, with results which were liable, as he had learnt before now, to be sometimes very different from the sum of their separate values.

There was, first, the light he had gained on Sir Daniel Denton's financial position. It removed one of the most frequent influences through which men who have no habit of fortitude may be disposed to their own destruction. It therefore reduced the probability of suicide, even apart from the more emphatic negative of the post-mortem evidence.

He saw also that the information he had gained rendered it improbable that Sir Daniel had been murdered by any member of his own family, with the object of financial advantage to themselves.

Like Mr. Wheeler, he had a momentary speculation as to whether Sir Daniel might not have deliberately endeavoured to commit suicide so that it would appear that he had died by another hand, which was a logical possibility if he had the terms of the insurance policy in mind, and were anxious to secure it for the benefit of his estate. That would imply, incidentally, that at the moment of self-destruction he must have had Lady Denton's interests at heart; and that, in its turn, would further narrow the range of possible motives, by eliminating that of any quarrel with her.

But, like Mr. Wheeler, he put the theory of a deliberately misleading suicide away as too fantastic in itself, and beyond serious consideration, at least so long as he could discover no motive which should have led Sir Daniel to contemplate suicide in any form.

The one conclusion at which he arrived definitely on these facts was that whatever had happened had not been inspired by financial considerations from any direction. As a murder motive, he could eliminate greed. What remained? Jealousy, hate, and fear.

His mind turned to the sinister hint which Mr. Redwin had uttered. If it were born of more than a baseless spite, it meant that something had happened in connection with his expulsion from Bywater Grange, or, at least, that something had been known to him which had led him to expect the tragedy. Or had he since done some overt act himself, of which it was an expected consequence?

Redwin was a man of whom he knew nothing good. He had been warned from two directions to discredit anything he might say. By his own statement, he was now actuated by the basest of human passions. Certainly he would not go far on his unsupported word.

But, in considering this, he must take account of the hint—it was scarcely less—that Mr. Fisher had given, that Redwin had tried to use his firm to exercise some pressure upon Sir Daniel to which the name of blackmail might be not inappropriately applied. He considered the various forms which this might possibly take, and though he had not the advantage of the information which Mr. Wheeler was receiving from Lady Denton at about this time, yet a wide experience of such activities caused him to include the exposure of income tax evasion, and the disclosure of compromising letters, among the probabilities of the case.

When he considered these, and the other facts which he had patiently accumulated during the day, as bearing upon the first question that he had come there to resolve—that of whether the warrant for Lady Denton's arrest should be allowed to be issued—he saw that, however vaguely, however slightly, the inferences against her had been increased. And he could see nothing new to be put in the opposite scale. At least, nothing beyond the fact that Mr. Wheeler had so robustly declared her innocence, and had thrown down a stake of £15,000 to declare the sincerity of that conviction. It was true that the money was not his own. But it was also true that it had been a voluntary offer on his part, and one which, it had been quite evident, had not been foreseen by the other side. This also must have its slight but definite influence on the judgment that it was his duty to form. But this judgment could do no more than point him in the right direction, so that he should not waste his time in efforts to construct a case against an innocent man—or woman. Evidence— definite legal evidence—such as can be proved in a court of law, was what he required, and of that he could not say that he had any more than Superintendent Trackfield's unimaginative methods had marshalled before he came.

The case against Lady Denton, which had seemed less than sufficient to the Chief Constable's mind, stood just where it did. He felt that, to justify himself, he must do something better than that.

Well, he would put it out of his mind now and get a night's rest. He would meet Mr. Wheeler at breakfast, and hear what he had to say. Mr. Wheeler was Lady Denton's solicitor. He was not likely to forget that. He did not expect that he would provide him with fresh evidence to prove her guilt.

But Mr. Wheeler knew the peril in which she stood, and if, after an evening which, the Inspector rightly guessed, would have been spent with her, he could make any suggestion which would direct enquiry away from herself, it was a thing which he would be certain to do.

CHAPTER XIII.

Mr. Wheeler talked on indifferent subjects. He said (with truth) that the soles were excellent.

He was alone with Inspector Pinkey, for breakfast had been brought on early to meet his convenience, and Lady Denton was not down. Gerard Denton's constitution was understood to be of that delicacy which requires its owner to have breakfast in bed.

The fact was that Mr. Wheeler had done some thinking during the night, and the more he considered Lady Denton's position, the less he liked it.

Even supposing that she had told him all the truth now (which he was quite sure she had not), there was a suggestion of possible motive, weak and ill-defined though it might be, yet sufficient, perhaps, to turn the scale with a jury of uncertain temper. If it came out, if the existence of those letters—letters which she had now destroyed—were to be disclosed, and that they were already brought, or about to be brought, to her husband's knowledge when his life was so abruptly taken, what ammunition would it not give to a prosecuting counsel? What deadly difference might it make to the summing up! His best hope lay in the fact that, if Lady Denton kept her mouth shut now (as she surely would), it was not easy to see how they would be disclosed. He decided that Redwin would find it difficult, if not impossible, to reveal their existence without incriminating himself more deeply than he would venture to do.

But he saw now that he had made a mistake when he had thrown that £15,000 into the scale. He ought to have gone all out for suicide, and let the bank and the insurance policy go by the board. And he must go all out for suicide now—unless the murderer could be found.

But he had no confidence in that. It was too great a risk, in view of the peril in which his client stood. Suicide it must be, and Sir Lionel Tipshift's opinion must go hang. After all, Lady Denton was not a poor woman. He knew that sufficient money would secure eminent experts to contradict each other on any subject under the sun. For a suitable retainer, Sir Lansbury Hopkins would give evidence, if desired, that Sir Daniel had been shot by a performing flea. Indeed, he would do it so plausibly that the jury would almost believe at the time, and wake up next morning to wonder why.

He had made a mistake about that £15,000, but he couldn't draw back now, if he would. It would be too significant that he should do so after interviewing his client. It would be like proclaiming his belief in her guilt. Besides, he was of the sporting temperament that will stand to any risk that has once been staked. To try to draw back now would be like hedging a bet.

He did not blame himself for the decision of the previous afternoon. How can any lawyer act for a client who does not instruct him fully? Even now—well, he must do his best for her, whether she had told all the truth or not.

But he decided that he must be very cautious as to what he should say to the Inspector. There were few aspects of the case which he could discuss without reserve. On the other hand, he must not appear afraid. Perhaps it would be best to say nothing directly concerning it during the first part of the meal—to let Pinkey bring it up if he would.

His strategy was so far successful that, when the meal was half over, the Inspector, who had his own reasons for desiring to talk on the subject which was in the forefront of both their minds, felt obliged to interrupt some remarks upon a famous draught in the Lord Chief Justice's Court, to say: "I don't want to worry Lady Denton more than I need, but there's some information I ought to have. I wonder whether you could tell me how it really was that Redwin left as he did, and if he were trying to blackmail her or Sir Daniel afterwards."

"Yes, I dare say I can tell you all that you need to know. He was dismissed for misappropriating shares, and falsifying the books he kept: systematic theft and forgery, without any excuse. He ought to be in gaol now, but I suppose Sir Daniel didn't want the worry and expense of a prosecution, as so many gentlemen don't.

"As to blackmail—well, it's a loose word, as we both l know, but I should say there's no doubt of that either."

"Did Lady Denton know that?"

"Yes, I've had it from her."

"Then I suppose you know what the ground of the blackmail was?"

"I'm not clear that I ought to say that. There are some things that may make a lot of trouble, if the idea gets about, even though they're quite false."

"You can trust my discretion not to give it any avoidable publicity."

"My difficulty is that I don't see what it has to do with Sir Daniel's death. If you could tell me that you're arresting Redwin for that, I should feel bound to tell you at once. But I don't see how you could."

"No, neither do I. I wish I did. But I should be glad to know what there is against him, if I find he's mixed up in it at all."

Mr. Wheeler, having got the information by that reply which he had himself been anxious to obtain without appearing to ask, now proceeded, as he had meant from the first, to impart one of those partial truths which he knew to be more potent for deception than many lies.

"It's a difficult position, but Lady Denton said she wished you to have all the help we could give, and I think I ought to stretch a point and trust you not to repeat it without more reason than there is now. It was when Redwin was being turned out. He said something in Lady Denton's hearing which she understood as a threat that, if he were not kept on, he would make disclosures to the Inspector of Taxes which would cause trouble to Sir Daniel.

"I dare say there wasn't a word of truth in it; or, if there were, I should say that Redwin, who kept the books and accounts, had done something wrong on Sir Daniel's behalf—perhaps without his knowledge at all—to get him into his power if he got found out, as he did.

"Sir Daniel treated it with contempt, and told him to go ahead if he wanted to end in gaol.

"I should be sorry for anyone who built a case on anything that man said or did. If you could make him responsible for Sir Daniel's death, it would be good news all round, but I don't see how you can."

"No," the Inspector said frankly, "neither do I. But I'm still hoping to find out a few things that I don't know yet."

"Well, you'll get any help from us that you like to ask. But I've been thinking over what passed at Fisher's office yesterday, and I've come to the conclusion that it's a case where the adjourned inquest ought to be held without more delay. I don't want to put that view to the coroner over your head. I thought I'd tell you first how it looks to me."

"I'm not quite sure that you're wrong," the Inspector answered. "And, anyway, I'm much obliged for the information you've given me about Redwin. It fits in very well with what I've heard from another source."

Mr. Wheeler felt that he had done rather well, and that the time had come when the conversation should be gently deflected to other subjects.

Inspector Pinkey saw that it was a possible thing that it was a question of income tax irregularity which Redwin had alleged against Sir Daniel in Forbes and Fisher's office, concerning which they had declined to act, though the threat with which he was said to have left them seemed to imply something rather different. For the moment, he might cease to enquire concerning that which he thought he knew, and the risk that he would learn of the stolen letters was reduced accordingly.

As to the inquest, it was the very proposal that he had intended to put to Superintendent Trackfield, if his own enquiries should fail to produce more than he had already learnt. Why should the police take the responsibility of a doubtful arrest, when the verdict of a coroner's jury might relieve them of it? Let the police inform the coroner that they did not wish the inquest longer delayed, and, if there were a verdict of suicide, the matter could be closed in that way. If there were one of murder against Lady Denton, she would be arrested on the coroner's warrant, and their responsibility would be nil. Even if the verdict were murder against some person unknown, they would be no worse off than they were today. Yes, if he could discover nothing more in the next forty-eight hours, let the inquest be held.

At the same time, the fact that Mr. Wheeler gave such advice led him to the natural deduction that he must feel a comfortable assurance of his client's ability to convince a coroner's jury of her own innocence. He could not guess that Mr. Wheeler, after making a £15,000 gesture of belief in the murder theory less than twenty-four hours ago, was now resolved in the privacy of his own mind to get the best counsel that wealth could buy to urge the alternative of suicide when the enquiry should be held.

He could not guess that the basis of his present decision was not confidence, but a lively fear that Lady Denton's case might not be improved by any further delay.

Meanwhile, Mr. Wheeler (with an anxious eye on the clock) was making some remarks on the uncertain value of circumstantial evidence, to which he was giving less attention than they may have deserved. Mr. Wheeler wanted to go. In ten minutes Lady Denton's car would be at the door. In twenty minutes his train would be due to leave the station at Beacon's Cross. Before leaving, he had wanted particularly to have a few words with the gardener's boy, by which he supposed (concerning which he was right in a way that he did not guess) the whole position might be transformed. And now, after what he had said, he could not move, either for garden or train, till Lady Denton should come down. For it had become vital to inform her that, if the Inspector talked of Redwin's blackmailing activities, he would be alluding to matters of taxation, and not to a lady's love letters, concerning which, while he was satisfied that he knew everything, he was not likely to enquire.

In about five minutes Lady Denton relieved his mind by walking into the room. In another five he was on his way to the station, after the necessary words had been spoken in a brief interview in the hall. But he had lost his opportunity of interrogating the gardener's boy.

CHAPTER XIV.

Inspector Pinkey had not completed his breakfast—indeed, had not intended to have completed it—when Lady Denton sat down.

Mr. Wheeler, reflecting complacently, as his morning express glided swiftly and smoothly through the London suburbs, on the power of the half-truth to deceive with greater safety and certainty than can be expected from any lie, might feel, with some reason, that he had had the best of the verbal skirmish with which he had started his business day. But he may have failed to consider the equal importance of the ancient proverb, *Magna est veritas, et praevalebit,* which was also destined to take a hand in the game.

Inspector Pinkey, carefully adjusting the facts he had previously assembled to the new ones which Mr. Wheeler had contributed, had no difficulty in believing that Redwin had threatened exposure of a taxation irregularity, nor in supposing that it was on that business that he had seen Messrs. Forbes and Fisher, and they had shown him the door. But, as he recalled his conversation with the discarded secretary, he was unable to accept this as a satisfactory explanation of the hint the man had given that he had anticipated Sir Daniel's death.

It is true that men have occasionally committed suicide under pressure of taxation difficulties, or when threatened with prosecution for discovered irregularities in the degree of their submission to the shearing process, but such a position had not arisen, even if Sir Daniel would have been likely to meet it in such a manner. Besides, had he been in a condition of desperate panic, he had an available remedy. He could have become reconciled to Redwin, which, however distasteful, was surely a milder solution than that which the pistol offered.

Redwin's statement might be no more than an empty boast, but if it had any basis of truth (as the Inspector was inclined to believe), it must be found elsewhere than in the incident which Mr. Wheeler had mentioned. The Inspector felt that there was still something he did not know. He resolved that he would make it his next occupation to give Mr. Redwin another visit, and, as he made the usual superficial conversational exchanges with Lady Denton, while these thoughts passed through his mind, he modified a previous decision to spare her the ordeal of further questions, and resolved that he would have the account of Redwin's departure from her own mouth.

It was fortunate for Lady Denton then that Mr. Wheeler had seen the importance of those whispered words in the hall, and had made opportunity to speak them. When the Inspector remarked casually that he had seen Mr. Redwin yesterday at the Station Inn, and asked, in an equally casual way, when and why Sir Daniel had turned him out, she knew that it was no more than Mr. Wheeler had told already, as he had had it from her.

She answered readily, and the Inspector had no difficulty in believing the tale he heard. But it did not follow that there was no more to be told. He asked, when she finished, in the same casual conversational way, not realizing, from long habit, the baseness of what he did: "Do you know whether Sir Daniel saw or heard any more of him after that?"

If there were anything to conceal, and he could have passed her guard, it was evident that the thrust had gone wide. "No," she said, instantly and frankly enough. "I don't think he did. But he didn't always tell me. No, I should say not."

She was silent a moment after that, and then added, in a more deliberate way: "I suppose you're trying to find anything that could connect him with what happened afterwards. Of course, I should be glad if you could. It would be worth anything to get it cleared up. But I think it's a waste of time, all the same. I don't see how he could have had anything to do with it, being so far away."

Was she telling the truth now? There was nothing in word or manner to suggest a lie. But there was a difference. She would talk sometimes in a frank, natural way, which was of an obvious and unstudied spontaneity, as she had done a moment ago. At others, such as these, she became, it seemed, consciously deliberate in the words she chose. What was the significance of the change? Inspector Pinkey, for all his experience, was not sure.

She was saying no more now than he heard from all sides, and had said himself—that it would be very satisfactory in itself to be able to connect Redwin with the crime (he seemed actually dressed for the part!), but it couldn't be done, and it was time wasted to try.

It had a sound of genuine advice from one who, if innocent, had so much to gain in security and peace of mind, if the murderer could be found; or, if guilty, could have no obvious motive in objecting to suspicion being directed elsewhere.

Inspector Pinkey saw that the advice had the apparent value of that which is against the interest of the one who gives it. Only if Lady Denton were more afraid of something that further questioning of Redwin would reveal than of the present suspicion under which she lay, could her words be interpreted as less innocent than they appeared. It was not a probable supposition, but he determined to investigate it further before he struck Redwin off the mental list of those to whom he still looked to contribute, willingly or unwillingly, to the solution of the problem he had in hand. He would be, as he had resolved already, at the Station Inn again before lunchtime came.

Lady Denton broke the silence, speaking again in her consciously deliberate manner: "Mr. Wheeler tells me that if it's decided that it was suicide, we may lose £30,000 of insurance money. It's a dreadful lot, and he wanted me to say that I can't believe it was that. But I can't see how it could have been anything else. So I told him, if he doesn't agree, he'd better not ask me about it at all."

"Yes," the Inspector said vaguely, "I suppose that's the best way." His mind was on the questions he could frame to make Redwin talk. But, in fact, Mr. Redwin was not disturbed that morning, and he had lunch alone, for Inspector Pinkey had found other business to do.

CHAPTER XV.

If we seek an ultimate cause, we must observe that Mabel was unable to speak clearly when she had a full mouth; and when she had failed three times to give the cook an articulate answer regarding the saucepans which should have been cleaned yesterday afternoon, we cannot wonder, from our previous observation of that excellent woman, that her voice rose in denunciation. *Inter alia*, she wanted to know where that dratted boy got the money to keep Mabel supplied with so many sweets during the past week.

Mabel offered no solution to this problem, which, indeed, she had not considered. She took the tributes her beauty brought (which Tommy had learnt should be something that could be sucked long, without the necessity for too frequent renewals in the midst of the washing up) without awkward enquiries as to how he was able to lay such gifts on her shrine.

But Inspector Pinkey, passing along the passage to go out by the side door, heard the question, and became suddenly aware that it was one which he might have occasion to ask in a more serious way.

Like a dog finding the scent, his body took a new alertness, and his step quickened as he went out on to the sidewalk; and, instead of following his first intention toward the gate, and ultimately to the Station Inn, he turned to the vegetable garden, where he had seen from his bedroom window, a few minutes before, that Mr. Bulger was clearing away the autumn wreckage of the kidney beans.

Mr. Bulger was in a very deaf but very affable mood. He replied so readily to several remarks that he did not hear, and with such misappropriate genialities, that the Inspector was encouraged to ask the direct question—how much was the weekly wage which compensated Tommy for his strenuous toil.

Mr. Bulger, after admitting that it was a good three miles to Loudwater by the upper road, heard the repeated question, and replied readily that the young varmint was getting twice what he was worth. Being invited to convert this answer into English coinage, he replied that it was nine shillings, to which he added the interesting though unsolicited information that his mother let him keep three pence a week for himself, except on those occasions when his father was out of work.

Inspector Pinkey asked no more of Mr. Bulger. He remarked that there was nothing like pulling the bean sticks up promptly, if they were to be used for another year, and having been assured in reply that the duck pond wasn't as low as it had been a month back, he departed in excellent spirits to make diplomatic purchases at the local sweetshops.

Before midday he had learnt that, on the Tuesday evening of the previous week, being the day on which Sir Daniel Denton's life had so abruptly ended, Tommy had purchased various sweets to a total weight of about three pounds from Mr. Cobbins' confectionery stores. His order had been of a varied character, consisting of a quarter of a pound from each successive bottle that pleased his eye, and when about half a dozen of these little parcels had been weighed out, Mrs. Cobbins had declined to proceed further until he gave her an ocular demonstration of his commercial stability. On that he had produced a one-pound note, and when the astonished lady had expressed a natural doubt as to how he could be in honest possession of such a capital, he had replied that it was a birthday present from an aunt at Ealing, she being a lady who wallowed in redundant wealth.

Inspector Pinkey would have given little for the wealth of that probably mythical aunt, but he felt that he himself had struck gold. He had an instant conviction that he would be able to return to London with a more exciting report than a mere endorsement of that which had been done already by the local police. He would have been less than human had he not felt a measure of elation in the fact that he had made discovery of that which had been overlooked by those who had been first over the ground. He may not have allowed sufficiently for the fact that they had not heard the clue proclaimed in the loud voice of the outraged cook.

He considered how best to garner the full fruits of his discovery, and he decided that Tommy should be interviewed suddenly, as he bent over his work, rather than summoned to the police station, and allowed time to think over the probable ordeal that would be before him.

But it was desirable that more than one should be present to hear the first confused replies, the possible lies or contradictions, with which he might attempt concealment of the source of his present wealth. He entered a street-side telephone box, rang up Superin-

tendent Trackfield, and invited him to meet him for lunch in half an hour's time in the nearby parlour of the Sandy Cow. He said he had an interesting piece of evidence to talk over relating to the Bywater Grange affair, but he would rather not discuss it over the phone. Superintendent Trackfield said that he would be there.

Half an hour later the two officers were seated at lunch together, and Inspector Pinkey narrated his morning's experiences.

Superintendent Trackfield agreed as to the probable importance of the discovery he had made. He quoted a favourite remark of an old police chief under whom he had served in his younger days, that you can often unlock a large door with a small key.

In the same spirit in which he recognized the probable importance of the discovery, he admitted the ability of the metropolitan officer. It was true that the discovery had its origin in the casual remark which he had overheard as he passed the kitchen that morning. That might be luck. But the idea which it had brought into his mind was the result of his own efficiency. He recognized the superior brilliance of the Yard technique with a generous measure of praise, which concealed some natural annoyance. He knew that, if this clue should prove as important as it promised to be, there would be reflections and comparisons made. And it was so easy to see now that he ought not to have accepted the boy's assurance so easily.

"I thought," Inspector Pinkey suggested, "that you might like to come with me when I question him, and then we'd follow it up together. Two heads are better than one, and so are two witnesses to whatever's said."

The Superintendent said that he would be pleased to come. Perhaps willing would have been a truer word. It could not give him much pleasure to play second fiddle on his own ground. He quite understood that Pinkey was to do the investigation, and it would be his part to stand by. But, all the same, it was his duty. And Pinkey deserved it too. He got up to come.

They found the boy planting out winter cabbages. He had something in his mouth that impeded speech. The cheerful grin on his face altered somewhat as the two officers approached, but was in fairly good working order by the time they were near enough to observe.

"Tommy, where did you get that pound note that you changed at Mr. Cobbins' shop on the Tuesday night of last week?"

"Me aunt sent it me."

The Inspector showed no surprise. He asked: "Was it the aunt over Maidenhead way, or the one at Rochester?"

The boy looked up sullenly. He knew that the Inspector was pulling his leg. He had no aunts.

"Tommy, who gave you that note?"

"It mighta been anyone."

"It might have been Mr. Gerard."

"I told yer I picked it up."

"We didn't hear that. Now, Tommy, you just listen to me. You've told lies enough, and another one might mean that you'll be locked up for the night. Why did Mr. Gerard give you that note?"

"I didn't say as 'e did."

"You didn't say that he didn't, which meant just the same. Had he given you one before?"

"No."

"Then why did he give you one on Tuesday evening last week?"

"He musta thought as 'e would."

"No doubt he did. And you were to keep your mouth shut as to what you'd seen. Did you see him shoot Sir Daniel?"

"A course not. I were down the bend a' the drive."

"But you saw him come out through the window after he'd done it?"

"He come out to speak to me."

"Then he came out twice."

The boy's silence was a sufficient answer. "We'll have a bit more to say to you later, Tommy." The two officers went on to the house. They desired to interview Mr. Gerard before he should be aware of the discovery they had made.

CHAPTER XVI.

Mr. Gerard Denton received his visitors with a surface of nervous affability which was too thin to conceal the antipathy which underlay it.

"We've come together to see you, Mr. Denton," the Inspector began, "because you made a mistake. You should have given him half a crown."

Mr. Gerard looked, and may have been, genuinely puzzled for a moment by this opening.

"If there's anyone I ought to give half a crown to...," he began vaguely.

"I mean the gardener's boy."

Comprehension came, and confusion with it.

"I suppose I can give the boy what I choose?"

Mr. Denton was aware, even as he uttered it, of the weak futility of the reply.

"It's not a question of what you choose to give the boy, but of what explanation you choose to give us. We've heard what he has to say." There was a good-humoured grimness about Inspector Pinkey in these crises of pursuit, such as that of a butcher who enjoys his job. He was apt to become quick and even epigrammatic in retort. The little awkwardness which he had felt on the first occasion when his hostess had suggested that she herself might be cast for the role of criminal would have disappeared very quickly had he once decided to regard her in that light.

Superintendent Trackfield who, up to this point, had been a silent learner of the methods of the central organization, which were reputed to be so superior to his own, thought it right to interpose the remark that Mr. Denton was not obliged to make any reply which would incriminate himself, but, of course, any explanation he could offer.

"The fact is, I got flustered. It was a silly thing to do."

The reply came in a somewhat more confident tone, responding to that of the warning he had received, but it was Chief Inspector Pinkey who resumed charge of the conversation.

"It's never wise to get flustered."

"I didn't mean that. I mean, it was silly to give the boy any money."

"It was silly to give the boy as much as you did. He's never stopped sucking sweets since he got it. Do you mind telling us why you gave him any at all? It's only fair to tell you, Mr. Denton, that we've had his account of the matter."

"Because he'd seen me come out of the window just before, and I didn't want to be mixed up in it more than I could help."

"He saw you come out through the window twice."

"Yes, but—"

"Then the statement you have already made is untrue?"

"Yes, but—"

"Should you like an opportunity of amending that statement? Suppose you call at the police station at seven this evening? That'll be a quiet time."

He did not look for a reply, and Gerard Denton understood that it was an order rather than an invitation. The two officers turned to go.

The Superintendent was inwardly rather surprised at the respite which this arrangement gave. "You feel sure he'll come?" he asked, as they went down the drive.

Inspector Pinkey was in a genial mood. He had some reason for that, having demonstrated his ability to the rural mind. He gave a ready explanation.

"Yes, he'll come sure enough. It's that or bolt. And if he bolts now, it's just like hanging himself. He'll spend the time making up some lie or other that'll do the job in another way."

"He'll try to get hold of the boy."

"Yes, but he won't succeed. That's partly why I put him off till evening. We'll take the boy back with us now, and have his statement first. We needn't let him leave till Mr. Gerard's walked in. It's another matter when he'll walk out, and where to."

The boy was still at work on the cabbage planting.

"Tommy," said Inspector Pinkey, "how long was it after the shot was fired that Mr. Gerard came out of that window? I mean the first time he came out."

There was a pause before the reply came. The boy seemed confused or possibly afraid, lest he might increase the depth of the pit into which he had fallen already. His eyes seemed to dodge those of the Inspector, to look past or beyond him. At last he said: "It wasn't after, it was before."

As he said this, Inspector Trackfield looked round, following the direction of the boy's glance. Gerard Denton stood a few yards behind them.

Whether it was that they had been absorbed in their own conversation, or that he had followed on slippered feet, or that he had trodden the grassy edging of the drive, or a combination of these circumstances, the fact remained that the vital question had been asked and answered with the boy under his own eye.

"Mr. Denton, you've no right....," Inspector Pinkey began angrily, and then checked himself. It was seldom, indeed, that he lost his self-control in such ways.

"I suppose I can walk in my own garden?"

The Inspector did not answer. He said to the boy: "You'd better put that trowel down and come with us."

CHAPTER XVII.

The two officers walked back to the station with Tommy between them, to the excitement and pleasure of the inhabitants of
Beacon's Cross, who watched their transit. Those who had a near
view could observe for the first time that his countenance, on which
the usual grin appeared to have been permanently replaced by an
expression of sullen stubbornness, was of a distinctly criminal type.
During the afternoon the rumour that he had done no more than take
a handful of one-pound notes from Lady Denton's handbag fought
in uncertain battle against that which saw him as the murderer of his
employer, swiftly and callously emptying his pockets (probably of
notes already marked for his undoing), while his victim lay in the
agonies of approaching death.

The police station was in sight, but not reached, when Tommy's
captors were obliged to turn to repel the attack of a breathless and
indignant mother, who had left her washing board in haste, on a
jeering and somewhat inaccurate statement being shouted at her by
some boys who ran past her door to the scene of drama, that Potty
Briggs was a-running her Tommy in.

Mr. Charles Briggs (opprobriously known as Potty, owing to
certain alleged eccentricities of conduct which we must not turn
aside to observe) was a local constable. He lived next door to
Tommy's house, and familiarity had bred so much contempt in the
mind of the angry matron that, had Tommy actually been in his
beefy hands, the High Street of Beacon's Cross might have wit-
nessed an assault which would not have been forgotten till the next
war, or probably beyond that.

As it was, her charge slackened, and her wrathful countenance
became somewhat abashed, as she saw that she was confronted by
two of the superior officers of the law. With a swift change of direction, she trained her guns upon the defenceless culprit whom she had
been intent to rescue a moment earlier, demanding to know what

extremity of evil conduct had brought that ignominy upon the name he bore.

It is improbable that she would have been satisfied by Tommy's sulky assurance that he hadn't done naught that he knowed, but Superintendent Trackfield took the situation firmly in hand. Treading, as it were, on his own quarter deck, in the High Street of the town he ruled, he recognized that this was an occasion on which his own authority must be asserted, and even Chief Inspector Pinkey must stand aside.

"Now, Mother," he said, with a firm though kindly grip on a buxom arm, "you know you mustn't make a scene here. I've no doubt Tommy's a good lad, and good lads don't come to any harm where he's going now. You go back and get some tea ready for him for five o'clock, and he'll tell you all about it when he gets home."

She withdrew reluctantly, having done nothing to lighten the gloom of her son's mind, to whose previous troubles was now added a sound conviction that there would be something quite different from tea in his mother's kitchen, when he had concluded a confession which he now saw that he was inevitably destined to make. The police station, which had seemed so dreadful a destination before, now presented itself to his imagination as a harbour of intervening peace.

"I don't know," Inspector Pinkey said, when he had been handed over to the temporary custody of Potty Briggs, and the two officers were alone together, "about letting him go home by five o'clock. I thought of keeping him till we'd got Gerard Denton here."

"I shouldn't say that it matters, when we've got his new statement signed. If Denton were foolish enough to try to see him before he comes here, he'd just give himself away by trying it on."

Inspector Pinkey considered that view of the matter, and allowed its force. He was in a mood at once generous, complacent, and energetic. He determined to attack the yielding problem again from another side by a second interview with Mr. Redwin before the time should come to interrogate Gerard Denton with the causes of his inopportune liberality. He hoped to obtain further facts that would enable him to frame his questions in the right way.

"I don't think," he said, "that you'll need any help here this afternoon. You'll turn Tommy inside out quicker than I should. You're better up in the breed. I think I'll stroll over and look at Mr. Redwin again." The Superintendent accepted this as a gesture generously meant, though it contained an implication which was no less distasteful because he was not sure that it was entirely unmerited. He recognized that it was owing to no effort of his that Tommy was under detention now. He had no doubt that the resources which he controlled would be equal to abstracting the truth from his reluctant lips.

Inspector Pinkey took the road to the Station Inn, from which he returned at about six P.M., intending to have a chat with the Superintendent upon his own experiences before it should be time for Gerard Denton to call. But when he observed, as he entered, that Tommy's mother sat, massive and frowning, on a bench in the charge room, he concluded correctly that the examination had not proceeded smoothly to its expected end, and that Tommy had not left in time to be home to tea. He must put his afternoon's experiences aside for the moment, for the consideration of the more immediate problem.

"I've kept him," Trackfield explained, "not that I think it's going to be any good, but because I thought you might like to have a try at him yourself. Anyway, it's your case now, and it's for you to decide whether we're to ask him to sign this."

As he spoke, he passed over a foolscap sheet on which Tommy's present statement had been transformed into the official jargon considered necessary for such documents.

Inspector Pinkey, glancing down it with practised eyes, observed that it was a free and voluntary statement on the part of the gardener's boy, in which he withdrew the one that he had previously made when examined on the day following the tragedy. He admitted that he had withheld part of the truth in accordance with a promise made to Mr. Gerard Denton, in return for which he had received a one-pound note from that gentleman. He now said that he had seen Mr. Denton come out of Sir Daniel's study not only after, as had been asserted previously, but also immediately before the shot was fired.

"And that," the Inspector said, "is no good to us."

"Well, he won't budge. We can't tell him that he's got to say that he saw Denton come out of the study window immediately after the shot was fired, whether he likes it or not, though I've no doubt that's what happened. He might turn round in the witness box, or the other side might suggest we'd got his evidence in the wrong way. I've gone as far as I dared, and everyone on the staff has had a try, but he just sits sullenly there and says that's what he saw."

"I said it's no good to us," Inspector Pinkey repeated, "against Denton, I meant. But it's worse than that. It means, if he withdrew it later, he'd be no use at all. His value as a witness for anything'd be about gone."

78

"It was Denton getting behind us there on the drive. He daren't tell the truth, with him looking on, and now he thinks it's best not to alter again."

"Yes," the Inspector agreed, with a frankness that took at least a share of the blame, though an impartial judgment might have set down a somewhat larger percentage to his account. "We were both mugs about that, if you ask me."

"Would you like to try him yourself?"

"Yes, I'll do that. But it doesn't sound as though it's going to be any good."

He spoke with a well-founded pessimism, for when, after dismissing his reluctant mother with an assurance that her son would be with her shortly after seven, but certainly not before, he settled down to Tommy's interrogation, he was met with a monotonous repetition of the statement which had been reduced to writing already.

There was one moment, however, when the long-badgered youth appeared to hesitate upon the verge of supplying the varied edition which his captors were so plainly anxious to have. But it appeared that, even at the point of surrender, he recalled something which hardened him to a continuance of his previous attitude, leaving the Inspector in some doubt of whether he had inclined toward a belated candour, or had been tempted to secure his immediate popularity by substituting whatever he felt they would like him to say for an actual memory.

Inspector Pinkey had no wish to fake evidence. His aim was to get at the truth in such a form as could be legally put forward, and he knew that it might often be reached by such patient persuasions as were being adopted now. Where there is a strong but legally unprovable presumption of what that truth may be, it is easy to go too far on persuasion's path.

He recognized that he was in danger of that excess, and he abandoned a useless effort, which he knew that some would say should have been done much earlier.

He left the boy with an instruction that he could be released as soon as Mr. Denton had been shown into the Superintendent's office, to which he now returned.

"The boy," he said, with some irritation, "is no use to us, except that he can't deny that Gerard Denton bribed him, whatever for, and that's the kind of fact that takes a lot of explaining away. I don't think we'll get him to sign that statement. It's no use to us, unless we decide that Denton comes clear, and then it seems to tie Lady Denton up in the same knot. If we let him sign it, it might be hard to keep it out of court, even if we'd proved it was lies from end to end before we'd be going before the judge.

"We can get him to sign it later, if we have reason to think it's true. That infernal sweep creeping up behind us as he did. I dare say the only trouble is that he's afraid of losing his job."

CHAPTER XVIII.

While the interrogation of the gardener's boy was proceeding at the police station, with results of such doubtful utility to the patient bloodhounds of the law, a conversation was going on at Bywater Grange which those persistent gentlemen would have been glad to hear.

It took place in Lady Denton's room, with Gerard walking distractedly from door to window, and his sister-in-law, who may have seen less reason to disturb her mind, more comfortably stretched on a couch which had been upholstered with the primary purpose of supplying an effective background for her own fair and intelligent head.

"You've brought it all on yourself," she said, without over much sympathy in her tone, "and it's no use fussing now. I told you at the time it was an absolutely crazy thing to have done, but it was half an hour too late then for sense to do any good."

"How could I tell...?"

"You couldn't. That was just it. When you're not sure what to do, it's mostly best to do nothing, and let other people make the mistakes."

"And suppose I do nothing now?"

"Well, you might do worse. They can't force you to go there, and when they bother you next, you can say that you thought it over, and decided to say nothing more."

"But I've signed a statement that they know now isn't right."

"No, they don't. It's just Tommy's word against yours. And he's told one lie already."

"Yes. And they know why."

"That's your own silliness, as it's no use saying again. But I don't see that you've got so much reason to fuss. You heard what Tommy said in the drive, and you'll tell them the same tale, and what good will that be to them?"

"Yes, if they don't get him to say something else."

"Why should he? Don't be a fool! And, if he did, he could change again, and what use would he be then?"

Gerard made no reply to this. He walked restlessly up and down, with an occasional "Damn the boy!" or other ejaculation of an unhelpful character. He glanced restlessly at the clock about once a minute, and it moved in the unemotional mechanical way that clocks will at the crises of life, until Lady Denton, who had been watching him in a very serious and considering manner, asked: "I suppose you've made up your mind to go?"

"Yes," he said. "You ought to see that I've got to go."

He knew in his heart that he would have to go, be it foolish or wise. He lacked the courage to stay away. But he had a better reason than that. He knew that Adelaide had been wrong when she had said that it was only Tommy's word against his. Had he not admitted to the police, in those first agitated moments, that he had given Tommy the money to lie? And wasn't that an admission that his own state-ment, having agreed with Tommy's, must have been false? He couldn't remember what he had said as clearly as he would have liked to do, but he knew he had admitted that, and he didn't see now how he could have done any differently. He must have admitted some reason for giving Tommy the money. But it was no use telling Adelaide about that. She would only sneer at him again.

In any case, he knew that he would be bound to go. The same nervous anxiety to be aware of the worst would be a substitute for courage to take him there, as it had led him to follow the officers when they had questioned Tommy that afternoon.

"Well," Lady Denton was saying, "if you've made up your mind to go, I'll give you one piece of advice. If you want the trouble to end here, you'll tell them the truth now."

"Tell the truth?" he exclaimed, as though in utter surprise or bewilderment at this advice. He stared at her with astonished eyes.

"I mean, tell them about the row."

"I don't see the need for that. I don't suppose Tommy heard."

"Neither do I. Gerard, haven't you got any sense at all? Isn't it the reason why you got frightened, and gave him the pound? They don't know that you don't think that Tommy heard everything that was said."

After this, he walked up and down in more agitation than be-fore. The advice seemed mad. And yet he wasn't quite sure it was wrong. He had a great respect for Lady Denton's ability, and he saw that she moved through the present trouble more serenely than he, though it had brought suspicion to both their doors. Was it because, if she did not exactly tell all the truth, she had practised a strict economy in the lies she used?

In any case, it would be the simplest way. Gerard Denton was well aware that there is less mental exertion required in supplying a truthful narrative than in sustaining a weak-founded lie. And even if you are telling something less than the whole—even something very much less—a leaven of fact gratuitously supplied, and especially fact which might seem adverse to himself, and could have been learnt from no other source...yes, Adelaide might be right, as she often was.

He glanced irresolutely at the clock again, and went to the cloakroom to prepare for the ordeal which his own folly had brought down on his most inadequate head.

CHAPTER XIX.

Inspector Trackfield looked at the clock.

"No," he said, in answer to the question he had just heard. "I should say it's about two minutes slow."

The two officers sat in the police station reception room, awaiting the presence of Mr. Gerard Denton.

The hands of the clock pointed to seven-oh-five.

As Inspector Pinkey made no reply, he added: "I wonder whether we oughtn't to have brought him in then, before we questioned the boy. We'd got enough on him to have held him for a few hours, if not more, while we thought it out. I did think of having a watch put round the house, but I didn't want to interfere, and you'd gone off to the Station Inn." The mention of that reminded him of the Inspector's purpose of having a few more words with Mr. Redwin. "You might tell me how you got on...I suppose we've got to give him to the half-hour."

Inspector Pinkey, having the benefit of a much more extensive experience in the incidence of such interviews, was unperturbed.

"It's no use starting that now. I don't suppose there'll be time. They're almost always a bit late. That's nervousness, I suppose. And they're never late more than a few minutes. I suppose that's nervousness, too. If they come on the tick, it's often best to let them sit waiting for half an hour. But I don't think we could have run him in on the mere fact that he gave a pound note to the boy. And if we'd made any charge, we should have had to caution him, and he might have said he'd shut up till he got legal aid. We're far best as we are, keeping open minds, and asking him to explain. And my mind's open enough. I've got no settled opinion yet of what happened in that room, or who was there when Sir Daniel died.

"Besides, if we had arrested him, where should we be now, with the boy sticking out in the way he does? You're often worse off when you've detained a man, and then let him go, than if you'd left him alone till you learned more."

"I dare say you're right. I'll agree to that, if he turns up. But if he tells the same tale as the boy, I don't see that we're much further advanced."

"But we've got one good card—the fact that he won't know what the boy's said."

"Yes, that's true. Especially if he's lying now."

The conversation was interrupted by the ringing of a desk telephone to announce that Mr. Gerard Denton had arrived.

The Superintendent, who took the call, gave an interrogative glance at Inspector Pinkey, from whom he got an affirmative nod, and said: "Show him up."

A minute later, Gerard Denton entered the room, and was invited in a formal manner to take a seat at some distance from the two officers, who had not risen.

Inspector Pinkey, crushing the end of a cigarette in an ashtray with firm extinguishing fingers, commenced the conversation after a style which had been successful on more than one previous occasion in obtaining confessions by which those who had taken the lives of others succeeded in hanging themselves, which it was improbable that anyone else would have been able to do. His method had an appearance of magnanimity, and may be compared, without unfairness to either side, to that of those who will hold back the hounds till the hare has sufficient start to give them all a good run—but not, of course, enough to let it get free.

"Mr. Denton," he said, "before I ask you to make any further statement, I want to put your position squarely before you, and, after that, if you have any explanation to offer, or wish to amend the statement you have already made, it will be for you to say. I don't suppose I need tell you that we only want to get at the truth, and we're not only willing, we are anxious to give full consideration to any facts in your favour that you can bring forward, just as much as those that tell against you that we already know."

Mr. Denton, so far from being grateful for this considerate opening, was roused to a flustered protest. To his mind, it had a very menacing sound, beyond that which he had expected to hear.

"You don't mean to say," he protested anxiously, "that you're accusing me of causing Sir Daniel's death?"

"I don't mean that I'm accusing you at all. If I were accusing you of murder, you'd be under arrest. If you'll listen, you'll understand what I mean, and after that you can talk as much as you like."

The attitude which he was adopting now was not an invariable custom toward those he might invite to give explanations of their proximity to events of crime. He would often be patiently persistent in the securing of written statements which must not only be signed at the end, but initialled on every page. But when you have a statement already filed which is admittedly false in a very damaging particular—well, you can afford to appear generously indifferent on the question of whether it shall be amended to something else, which may or may not be nearer the truth than it is now.

On this occasion, somewhat to Superintendent Trackfield's unexpressed surprise, the Chief Inspector did not even suggest the presence of a shorthand writer, nor the provision of the usual official foolscap, on which an amended statement might be neatly and skilfully rendered into the police vernacular. He did not comment on these omissions, preferring to observe in silence the technique of the central organization, and he was to feel some satisfaction in this reticence when he received a subsequent explanation of the Inspector's procedure, which he would find to be special to this occasion rather than a formula of routine. But that explanation was not to come until Gerard Denton's ordeal was over.

At the present moment, Mr. Denton sat in an obvious discomfort, which he vainly sought to control to such semblances of indifference or indignation as he considered the more suitable front to present to the discharge of the Inspector's batteries.

"The position you have to face," Inspector Pinkey went on, in the reasoning tone of one who points out to his fellow man a danger into which he may heedlessly fall, "is that, on your own statement, when your brother was murdered—as we are assured that he certainly was—you were the first on the scene, excepting only Lady Denton herself, and must therefore have been at no great distance away when the crime was committed.

"You came, you said, from the library, where you had been reading, and Lady Denton's evidence confirmed this. In her evidence, it is stated also that she crossed the passage so immediately after the shot was fired that it would have been a physical impossibility for the murderer to have left the study and passed along the passage to the library without being seen by her.

"But we have less certain evidence that you would not have had time to leave the study by the window after the shot was fired, and before Lady Denton entered, and to have returned to the library; or, at least, to have entered the house, and come back to the study by the passage when Lady Denton cried out. It is, indeed, evident that you could have done this, and answered her call almost immediately.

"But to observe a possibility is very different from proving a fact, and—until today—we had the statement of the only available witness, the gardener's boy, in support of your own account. We have now learnt that that evidence was untrue, and, on your own admission, you had bribed the boy to deceive us. It is in accordance with our usual practice that we invite you to offer any explanation you may desire, or to amend your previous statement in any particular, before we draw the natural inferences from what we have just learnt. But there is no compulsion upon you to do so. It is a matter entirely for your own decision, bearing in mind that you have admitted the bribery of the boy."

"I said I gave him the note. We often do silly things when we get upset."

"No doubt we do. But it's not the question of whether it was wise or foolish that concerns us now, so much as the reason why it was done."

"There wasn't any real reason."

"Wasn't it so that he might deceive us as to what he had seen?"

"I didn't ask him to say anything that's not true."

"Perhaps not. But I suppose you know what *suppressio veri, suggestio falsi* means?"

"I didn't want to be mixed up in it more than I need. No one would."

"Then you admit that you were mixed up in it?"

"I mean, having come out just before."

"Before what?"

"Before he was shot."

"Mr. Denton, I want to be fair to you, but the argument is not easy to follow. If, as you apparently wish us to believe, you were seen to come out of the study window just before the murder occurred, it doesn't show you to have been mixed up in it at all. It seems to show, so far as it goes, that you weren't there."

"Well, I wasn't. That's what I've always said."

Mr. Denton perceived by the Inspector's expression that he did not consider this reply entirely adequate. He remembered Adelaide's advice, which had sounded so foolish when it was given, but had a more possible aspect now. He added: "I'd just had a row with Daniel. I didn't want that to come out. I thought it wouldn't sound very well. So I didn't want anything said about my having been there at all."

The Inspector heard this surprising admission with an expressionless face, though he supposed that it marked the advance of another of the short, slow, hesitant steps which will lead to the truth at last. He only asked: "What was it about?"

"It was always the same thing."

"Money?"

"Yes. It was the way he doled it out."

"And how did the row end? Did you get what you wanted?"

"Partly. I wanted eighty pounds. I got twenty-five."

"Was it cash or cheque?"

"It was a cheque. Mr. Wheeler's got it now."

"Mr. Wheeler? Why?"

"I didn't know whether I should get it paid after Daniel was dead, so I took it to him. He said I'd better not present it, but, if I liked, he would give me the money."

"Then Mr. Wheeler knew all about this quarrel?"

"No. I only told him I'd got a cheque that I wanted to cash."

"And I understand that you get control of your own money, now that your brother's dead?"

"Yes, I hope I shall."

"Do you mean you don't know?"

"Mr. Wheeler says he thinks I shall. It's a question of whether another trustee'll be appointed, and he says there's no power under the will, but he'll have to go to the court for directions."

"Did you know this before?"

"I hoped I should get it, if Daniel died. But I didn't know. I don't know much about law."

"I see. Mr. Denton, I'm not saying I believe you or not. But I'm not going to ask you to sign another statement tonight. I suggest that you should think over your position very carefully, and come and see us again, say on Monday evening. You ought to be very careful, if you amend your statement, that you get it right this time. A habit of making false statements, when you've been as close to a murder as you have to this, would be very dangerous for yourself."

Mr. Gerard Denton went out. He was surprised, puzzled, confused, at the way in which the interview had so abruptly ended. Vaguely, he felt that Lady Denton's advice had been instrumental in leading up to that unexpected dismissal, and that he owed her some thanks for that. But he reflected that, when the whole circumstances, as they were known to both of them, were reviewed, it was no more than a sister-in-law should be expected to do.

He left behind, in Superintendent Trackfield, a man as surprised as himself, but one in a better position to relieve this sensation by direct enquiry.

"You don't think," he asked, "that a new statement's worth taking?"

"I don't think there's any hurry."

"I suppose not, while the boy stands to the same tale."

"I didn't only mean that. I'm not sure that he isn't telling the truth."

"And, if so, it makes it almost certain that Lady Denton did it?"

"Yes. It makes it worse for her than it was before. It makes it almost sure, but not quite. But the first question is whether to believe Gerard Denton or not."

"He's lied once. You can't easily trust a man after that."

"Yes, but not more than the average man, if he found himself in such a hole, might be expected to do, and there's a certain simplicity about the way he does that—and the way he tells the truth, if it is the truth—too."

"You mean about the row he had with Sir Daniel just before he was shot?"

"Yes, that particularly. Wouldn't a man who had more to hide have hidden that too? But you never know. I've learned never to be surprised."

Superintendent Trackfield was disposed to agree with this somewhat qualified belief in Mr. Gerard Denton's probable innocence. But it is to be observed that neither of these intelligent officers was aware that the course of his admissions had been suggested by another mind.

But the Superintendent, at the risk of being thought more stupid than he supposed that he really was, continued the admission of his own bewilderment, and his frankness was again rewarded.

"I still don't see," he said, "why you put him off till next Monday night."

"No, I don't see how you could. I must have seemed rather a fool to you. I didn't have time to tell you before, between questioning the boy and Gerard Denton being due. It was the talk I had with Redwin this afternoon.

"We've got nothing on him that we can use, though we expect he's a blackmailer and know he's a thief; and, as to this murder, I'm no nearer connecting him with it than I was before; but I don't think I've ever met a man that it would give me a greater pleasure to lay by the heels, if I could see how.

"The fellow hints at things that he won't say, and I've got an instinct that it's something more than just bluff. He knows something that he'd give any soul he's got to blurt out, if he could do it without hanging himself. That's the impression he gives me.

"So I hinted a bit too. I gave him a hint that some things might be overlooked if they were disclosed in the right way, and to enable us to deal with something else of a more serious kind, that would be regarded very differently if we should find them out for ourselves.

"I don't know how much effect it had. He only made some sneering reply about what we found out for ourselves not being much. He'd been rude enough before then. 'I notice you fellows never bark so loud as when you're under the wrong tree,' was one of his contributions to the conversation. But I let all that pass as though I had a deaf ear. I dare say our time will come. It mostly does with his sort.

"But whether it was the hint I gave, or just that his hatred of someone—whoever he wants us to think it is—was too strong to endure the thought that he might go free, I can't guess, but between the two he ended up by saying that, if we were still hunting round on a cold scent, I could see him again on Monday afternoon, and he might show us the vermin we want to catch."

"And you think he can?"

"I wouldn't say that. I don't trust him a yard. If I wasn't so clear that a man can't shoot another when he's playing billiards two miles away, I shouldn't be oversure that he hadn't put me off till Monday to allow good time for a getaway for himself. But I thought I'd put Denton off till the evening of that day, so that he'll come here without being specially summoned, just as soon as I've found what Redwin's wanting to spill. By the way, what proof did you have, beyond it being at the bottom of Denton's trunk, that it wasn't his gun with which Sir Daniel was shot? I mean, why shouldn't Denton have taken Sir Daniel's gun out of his drawer after he was shot and put it into his own trunk?"

The Superintendent admitted that he couldn't say.

CHAPTER XX.

Inspector Pinkey, reviewing the events of the past day, during a somewhat wakeful night, was conscious of a feeling of dissatisfaction, for which he told himself in vain that there was no adequate cause.

The day had, indeed, been one of active progress and unexpected discovery. The disclosure of the bribing of Tommy, and the admissions that his statement and that of Gerard Denton were deliberately inaccurate, were an important, and might be an essential, step toward the solution of the whole enigma. Beyond that, he had the hint from Redwin which, obscure as it was, might yet prove to be the pointer which would guide him to the evidence he required. And he had Redwin's promise that he would give him further information if he should ask for it on Monday next.

Altogether a good day's work, and one which had taken its catch from waters where the local police had fished vainly before. But the Inspector's trouble was that he could not see what to do next. The information which he had gained, significant and potentially serious though it might be, was not enough in itself to fasten the crime upon any one of those it concerned, nor did he see how it could be used for the obtaining of further, more decisive, evidence.

If the evidence of Tommy and Gerard Denton, as they now agreed upon it, could not be shaken, it definitely cleared Gerard Denton, if not of any participation in the crime, at least so far that the fatal shot could not have been fired by his hand. If that evidence were accepted as true, it definitely—some might say decisively—increased the gravity of the suspicion attaching to Lady Denton.

But, even so, it did not follow that it would make a conviction easier to obtain, for the case against her would now largely rest on the evidence of two witnesses who had discredited themselves in advance, and whose unsupported testimony a jury would be very slow to accept.

Besides—quite apart from what a jury might or might not be induced to swallow, the vital question remained—was Gerard Denton telling the truth now, or simply offering an amended lie? It was a vital question to the Inspector, for though, when he made an arrest, he liked a conviction to follow, he liked also to feel sure that he had laid his hand on a guilty man.

And apart from this, there was Redwin's promise. But the Inspector neither wished to avail himself of it, nor could he feel confident that it might not lead him further astray. The way in which it had been offered had been an insult hard to endure, with its suggestion that the evidence was lying under his eyes, but that he must first prove his incompetence before Redwin would contemptuously come to his aid. The spirit which underlay it was of an obvious malice, from one of less than doubtful integrity. Yet he knew that it was upon such sources that he must often rely, from such motives that the insinuations were often made by which he would obtain the convictions of better men than the informers from which they came.

When he reviewed the past day, he felt that he had done well; when he considered the one which was near its dawn, he could not see what he should do next. Perhaps a chat with Mr. Fisher, if he could make a pretext for that. Perhaps a few further words with Mr. Gerard. Or with Lady Denton at breakfast time. Perhaps something would occur, such as had done yesterday, when he had overheard the voice of the angry cook.

With these thoughts he fell asleep at last, and waked to see, by the pattern of pale October sunshine upon the wall of his room, that it was somewhat after the usual hour at which he was accustomed to rise.

He dressed in some haste, and descended to find Lady Denton already seated at the breakfast table.

She greeted him with a serene cordiality, seeming oblivious, as she always would, of the sinister cause which had brought him there; and he had a passing thought of admiration, akin to wonder, at the pose and self-control of her attitude, which he was able to contrast with that of others whom he had met under more or less similar circumstances. Courage—nerve—breeding—*mens sana in corpore sano* (he was rather fond of Latin proverbs)—came to his mind. He saw qualities that he could recognize and admire. But the vital question—were they signs of a serene innocence, or of such character as would not shrink from an act of crime?—was beyond decision, leaving him in no more than an equal doubt.

Yet he saw that the foundations of this attitude, whatever else they might be, were not mental obtuseness, nor were they the product of a strong-willed effort to put her husband's death, with all its attendant circumstances, out of her mind. He remembered that she had introduced it as a subject of conversation before, as she was to do now, when, with a smile of disarming pleasantness, as she passed his coffee, she made the surprising remark: "I'm afraid, Inspector Pinkey, you're not making yourself very popular in this house."

The Inspector, like most men whose hair is of the colour which Gerard Denton disliked, was not easily abashed or discomfited, but he felt a moment's uncertainty of how to take this remark, or in what tone to reply. He had never been quite sure that he should have accepted Lady Denton's invitation, and though his decision had been justified by results, for his discoveries of yesterday might not otherwise have been made at all, yet that very success was productive of its own embarrassments, which might increase as the hours passed. And now he had the feelings of one who has been politely told that his manners are not good enough for the table at which he sits.

"I am sorry," he said. "I suppose I shouldn't have come. But after what I learned yesterday, which, of course, I couldn't have foreseen, it was in Mr. Denton's own interest to ask him to give any explanation he could. I have to thank you for the hospitality you have shown to one whose presence cannot have been entirely pleasant. I shall be going within an hour."

Lady Denton listened to this apology with no more expression than a slight amusement in her eyes, but at the last statement she paused in the act of sugaring her coffee, with the tongs in her hand, as she asked: "You are going back to London today?"

"No," he said. "I thought it might be best if I moved to the inn."

"Because of what I said now? Of course you won't. I shouldn't have spoken at all if I'd meant that."

The Inspector had no difficulty in following the meaning of this somewhat enigmatical sentence, but he did not feel disposed to alter his decision.

"It's very kind of you," he replied, "but I still think that I'd better go."

"But you're quite wrong as to what I mean. I wasn't thinking of Gerard at all. Of course, he was rather sulky when he came back, having been kept away from his dinner till nearly nine. He got worse when he found that I hadn't waited. But it was silly to think I should. You might have kept him all night, for anything I could tell. But there's nothing fresh about that. He's been all sulks from the day you came. He won't see that it's best to get the thing cleared up properly. And as to last night, I told him he brought it on himself, if ever a man did. When I first heard of that pound, I told him that any lunatic asylum would put him up by himself, so that he shouldn't make the other patients worse than they were before."

"It was an exceptionally silly thing to do."

"Yes, that's what Gerard is. That's why his father left his money in Daniel's charge."

"And I suppose that naturally led to friction?"

"Yes. Daniel rubbed it in more than he need. I think he enjoyed seeing Gerard squirm. Did he tell you of the quarrel they had just before—before Sir Daniel was shot?"

"Yes, he told us about that."

"Then he took good advice for about the first time since he came to live with us here."

"You mean it was what you had advised him to do?"

"Yes, it was common sense. You never know where you end if you get tangled up in a lot of silly lies, and keeping back things that are best said. And this matter's too serious for such muddles.

"Whatever the truth is, Sir Daniel didn't shoot himself, or get shot, because he'd quarrelled with Gerard about his money half an hour before, as they did once a fortnight, more or less, so long as I've known them together. But if Gerard were silly enough to make a mystery about it, people might think anything. It'd be asking for trouble that he'd be most likely to get."

"Yes, you may be right about that. But if my unpopularity extends beyond Mr. Denton, I'm afraid I must have caused offence of which I was unaware. Have I been annoying the cook?"

"No, it's not quite that serious. The cook's sacred in this house!" The lightness of Lady Denton's tone faltered a moment as the words brought back to her mind the quarrel the woman and Sir Daniel had had just before his death, but she quickly recovered herself as she went on: "It isn't even Tommy, though I dare say his opinions of you wouldn't place you among the saints. But I can't say anything about that. He wasn't seen here yesterday after you walked him off between you, without even telling Bulger that he wouldn't finish his job. It's Tommy's master who's got his knife into you."

"Because I interrupted the cabbage planting?"

"So Bulger reports. His language can be forcible when he's really moved. And no one can enjoy answering back, because he'll only hear what he wants."

"I thought of taking a stroll round the gardens this morning. I've got one or two things that I need a quiet time to think out. I'd better take the opportunity of apologizing for the trouble I've caused."

"Well, it's at your own risk. You've been warned." She added, in a more serious tone: "But you understand that there is no reason for you to move to the inn, if you're comfortable here."

"Yes, thank you. I'm sorry I misunderstood."

He was not sure that he ought to have come to that house, but, being there, he had realized, while he talked, that he ought not to withdraw unless he had more evidence against one or other of its inmates than he had yet been able to obtain. To do so now would have an evident implication to the minds of all who were aware of the errand that brought him there. He could not tell whether Lady Denton had the same thought, or that, if he went to the inn, it might bring him into closer contact with Redwin, which she might not desire; but he saw that she could not have spoken with any considered purpose of causing him to withdraw from the house.

The thought of Redwin reminded him that he had a half-formed purpose in his mind of asking a sudden question, the reply to which might possibly give him some key to the nature of the secret which he professed to hold; but, from a confusion of disinclinations, he felt that he could not spring a trap of that kind immediately after the conversation that had just closed.

As he strolled out to the garden and considered the conversation, he was led to observe that Lady Denton's conduct toward himself had been beyond criticism, under conditions of more than ordinary difficulty. She had treated him with a friendly politeness, but had made no attempt to influence or cajole. She had given him the hospitality of the house, but had taken no advantage of that position, even to probe him with questions such as might be prompted by natural curiosity, even apart from the suspicion which she knew to be pointed against herself. He concluded that, if she were a murderess, she was also a singularly astute woman, and to murder a husband, unless under most exceptional circumstances, is something which an astute woman would be most unlikely to do.

CHAPTER XXI.

"I'm sorry, Mr. Bulger, I had to take Tommy away from his work yesterday afternoon."

For once, the ancient gardener appeared to hear without difficulty. "What you has to do, sir, you has; and I don't say but that'll take you through at the last day, if so be you can make it good.

"There's some maybe as thinks Tommy's worth harking to when he speaks, and there's some have known him a bit longer than you who'd give him a clout over the jaw, and tell him to mind his job. *Even a fool is accounted wise when he openeth not his mouth.*"

This somewhat surprising quotation, which is never likely to be popular at police headquarters, nor enscrolled over the entrances of judicial courts, must be attributed to the fact that Mr. Bulger combined his gardening activities with the position of local preacher for the Primitive Methodist denomination. In this office, his deafness was of no particular disadvantage, his habit of sometimes singing the wrong hymn (the number of which had been announced by an attendant deacon) only producing acute difficulty when he selected one of longer stanzas than that upon which his congregation had previously concentrated.

He was actually a preacher of considerable power, with a vein of humorous shrewdness which his hearers appreciated no less because it was an infrequent ingredient in the discourses on which they relied to save their souls from eternal fire. He was accustomed to mature these addresses during the long mental leisures allowed by the drilling of seeds, and the unhurried guidance of an electric mower. Long years of use had reduced most of his occupations to a mechanical though expert routine, leaving his mind free for the abstract verities, in the expounding of which his duty and pleasure met; and he may have been the only human creature in Beacon's Cross whose life fulfilled its own capacity and was entirely enviable.

The text of his sermon would be most commonly suggested by some experience or incident of the week, and the one he now quoted had been appropriately selected, even before Tommy's abduction had enriched the subject under at least four additional headings. There was an amount of inevitable gossip in the village, concerning both Redwin's departure and Sir Daniel's death, mostly of a fictitious, and some of a malicious, character, which was naturally resented by those who ate the bread of Bywater Grange, and the purveyors of scandal were to be chastised with vigour from the rostrum of the Primitive Methodist Chapel.

Inspector Pinkey was less able to appreciate the position than the Superintendent would have been, having less knowledge of local politics; but he observed that Mr. Bulger resented the fact that he had lost Tommy's help for the afternoon, and, more doubtfully, that he might be hinting that any statement the boy might make would be too unreliable to be worth the trouble it took to get. He answered amiably: "Well, we didn't get overmuch when he opened his."

Mr. Bulger again permitted himself to hear, and condescended to reply: "There's them as is that innocent they'd sup a puddle, and look to be drinking beer." He turned his eyes directly upon the Inspector, and there was a look in them almost of rebuke as he asked: "Why don't you give him a couple of pounds, and tell him what you want him to say?"

Inspector Pinkey felt confirmed in his conclusion of the night before that he had gone as far as wise, if not a step further than that, in endeavouring to persuade the boy to amend a tale, in the truth of which he had not believed. For, if Gerard Denton had come out of the study window before the shot was fired, why should he have bribed the boy to conceal a circumstance which relieved him from suspicion rather than cast it upon him? Even his own explanation, that it had been occasioned by his reluctance to mention the preceding row, or that it had been the folly of a flustered man, hardly seemed adequate in excuse.

But while the Inspector had sought only to get the truth from a difficult witness, who had admittedly lied before, he saw that his action might be construed in an opposite way. He had seen the danger already that a position might arise in which the boy would be a most vital witness, and yet in which he would be so disparaged that his evidence would be of little value to either side. He was glad again that he had deferred taking a second statement from him, till he were more assured that it would be a final one also.

He saw that Tommy must now have given his own version of yesterday's experience to Mr. Bulger, and the impression which it had made was expressed in that sarcastic query: "Why don't you give him a couple of pounds, and tell him what you want him to say?"

He saw also that there was an implication, whether deliberate or not, that Tommy's witness, having been bought once, could be bought again. He had to ask himself how far that might be true. So far, he had thought less of the question of Tommy's actual veracity than of how it might be made to appear in a court of law. But if he were fundamentally mendacious, it followed that there was no reliable witness as to who might or might not have come out of the study window before or after the fatal shot.

And the latter impression was not lessened as Mr. Bulger, appearing oblivious of the manner and deaf to the wording of this rebuke, went on, as though he talked to the raffle of the marrow bed that he was clearing away: "There's some as does their own work, as the Lord ordered they should. *In the sweat of thy brow shalt thou eat bread.* And there's others as does naught. *They toil not, neither do they spin.* And if the Lord sees they're not burdened with any brains, I won't say but He'll pass them through. But there's them as does naught worth doing themselves, and stops others that might, and what their end is most like to be is a thing we may think, if we don't say."

The Inspector had no difficulty in connecting this ominous reflection with his own responsibility for removing Tommy from the cabbage-planting activities of the previous afternoon, but he was less certain that Mr. Bulger's moody forecast of his own probable end was solely due to that delay.

Feeling that nothing would be gained by further attempts at conversation, but that he had some additional subject for reflection, though it might be no more than an added doubt, he left the precincts of the frost-spoiled marrows, and found a more comfortable location where a lawn-side seat was sheltered from the cool autumnal wind, and took the warmth of the mounting sun.

Sitting here, he considered how far it might alter the problem he had to solve if he should reach the conclusion that Tommy's evidence, whatever tale he might now tell, was entirely worthless, as Mr. Bulger clearly wished him to think.

It introduced the possibility that Tommy might have seen someone other than Gerard Denton leave the study window after the shot was fired. In that case, the key to the whole problem lay in the boy's mind; and, whether he could be persuaded to speak or not, it followed that enquiries should be made on a wider basis than he had yet commenced. He saw—he had, of course, seen from the first—

that the baffling limitation of the problem had always depended upon Tommy's statement that no one had left by the window after the shot was fired, until Gerard Denton came out. Had he not been there, it would have been a major probability that the murderer had escaped in that direction before Lady Denton entered the room.

But to consider that the boy was now guilty of such concealment introduced almost insuperable difficulties, which might not have been present had the presumption occurred at an earlier stage of the investigation.

Mr. Bulger was clearly loyal to his employers, on whom he could not fail to see that suspicion concentrated. If he should suspect the boy of concealing knowledge which would clear them, why should he discourage his examination, and suggest in advance that anything he might say should be disregarded? It was not probable that he was so greatly concerned to protect some outside individual, that he preferred that Gerard or Lady Denton should be accused of the crime.

And even if that possibility be allowed, it did not explain why Gerard should have bribed the boy—the one certain admitted fact—to the same end. Had he been bribed to say that some mythical murderer had run from the window after the shot had caused him—as it must have done—to look up toward it, it would have been a more rational procedure, however foolish.

No. Always putting aside the possibility of suicide, the bribery of the boy, and the present attitude of Bulger pointed the same way, and that was toward the wife and half-brother of the murdered man. One or other or the two in possible collusion?—must be responsible for the crime.

Coming to this commonsense, but somewhat reluctant, conclusion, he saw that suspicion was directed upon them in an exasperatingly almost equal degree. Previously, the logical deductions had seemed to be that Lady Denton had fired the shot, and, to the mind of Superintendent Trackfield, her arrest had been an inevitable consequence, from which only her reputed character and social position had precariously saved her, at least for a sufficient time for him to confirm the unwilling judgment of the local police. Now, the fact that Gerard Denton had bribed the boy had appeared for a moment fundamentally to alter the problem, and brought him under a strong suspicion, from which Lady Denton's own account of the matter had seemed to relieve him before. If that account were true, it had appeared clear that he could not have been on the scene of the crime; if it were false, its falsehood proclaimed her guilt. But if the boy's first account could not be believed, and as he had been bribed by Gerard to lie, the possibility that Gerard had left the window after committing the murder became an alternative solution which it was impossible to ignore. And, if that were so, and Bulger suspected it, if he did not know, it might account more plausibly for his willingness to discourage further pressure upon the stubborn reticence of the boy. But, if that were admitted to be the larger probability, how could it be established while the boy persisted in his present tale?

He saw at last that his conclusion led no further than this: the shadow of suspicion was almost wholly upon Lady Denton and Gerard, and in almost equal degree. Very slightly, it had shifted from her to him. But in the establishment of a legal case against him, he could not see that he had much progress to boast. The suspicion against either remained a measure of protection to the other which he saw no way to remove.

There still remained—he must not forget that—the possibility of some revelation from Redwin which would put him definitely upon the murderer's track. But it was not a possibility which gave him much pleasure or much hope. He was prepared, in the first place, for the promised information proving to be no more than an accusation of some criminal evasion of income tax liability, such as he supposed had formed the substance of the communication to Messrs. Forbes and Fisher, which had led to his being shown the door of their respectable offices. But he thought it unlikely, for several reasons, that it could be that and no more.

He did not dismiss the probability that fear of exposure and possible prosecution on such an accusation might cause men of exceptional emotional instability to put an end to their lives. But he did not think the proposition that Sir Daniel had done so from such a cause, and in the manner of his death, was worth serious consideration. Nor did he suppose, either, that Redwin would have such an opinion, nor that he would be anxious to communicate it to the police. It was far more likely that he desired to fix the guilt of murder upon someone against whom he had a real or imagined cause of animosity, as he was known to have against Lady Denton, who therefore became the most probable target for the attack.

But the very fact of this admitted animosity would render it necessary to consider any suggestion he might make, or evidence he might offer, in a very critical spirit; and the known character of the man would further discount it in the judgment of an impartial mind. The contemptuous insolence of the manner in which it had been promised rendered the Inspector additionally unwilling to avail himself of it, if he could obtain it—supposing it to be of a valid kind—from a cleaner source, and by his own deductions or investigations.

A combination of these motives, more or less consciously recognized, joined with a natural desire for action, where its direction was not otherwise clearly indicated, to suggest to his mind that he should do that about which he had hesitated at the breakfast table, and ask Lady Denton a direct question as to what Redwin might have against any inmate of Bywater Grange, apart from the alleged taxation irregularity, of which Mr. Wheeler had told him already.

He recognized that it would be, under a variety of possible circumstances, a mistaken method to question potentially guilty persons in such a way as to forearm them against attack, but, under those with which he now dealt, he decided that it was not only defensible, but might be considered the one most consonant with the best traditions of the service to which he belonged. He saw also that Lady Denton's reaction to such questioning, and the nature of her replies, even though they might be of a generally negative character, would be of a possible value in estimating the veracity of whatever statement the man might subsequently make.

It is only fair to the Inspector to consider these arguments at their true value, in the light of the position as he then knew it to be, rather than to judge them in the light of subsequent consequences, some of which would remain unknown to himself, even after he had brought the investigation to a conclusion satisfactory to the official mind, and had become busy with other things.

He decided to question Lady Denton further at lunch, and dozed pleasantly in the increasing warmth of the morning sun, and the natural consequence of a restless night.

CHAPTER XXII.

The lunch gong, sounding musically over the lawn, caused the Inspector to wake to a startled consciousness that his morning doze had been somewhat longer and sounder than was entirely creditable to a detective officer in the midst of an investigation that he had failed to solve. He went hurriedly into the house, and, not yet feeling entirely awake, was soon seated at the luncheon table at Lady Denton's right, and with her brother-in-law opposite to him, as they had been at the first dinner three days before.

He was not surprised to observe that, while Adelaide Denton retained her usual serenity, Gerard was obviously sulky and ill at ease in his presence. It was surprising, rather, after the ordeal of the previous evening, and he being what he was, that he should have come to the table at all. The Inspector could not know that a sharp word from Lady Denton had been needed to bring him unwillingly to his place, after the unwelcome intelligence that he was spending the morning beside the lawn, and would presumably be in for the midday meal. The expression on Gerard's face, and the constraint which Lady Denton endeavoured vainly to break with some remarks of a light inconsequence, reminded him of the assurance of his unpopularity which he had received from her at the earlier meal. It was a condition arising too frequently in the course of his investigations, being, indeed, inevitable, from the nature of the work that he had to do. He had learnt before now that, if he were to allow himself to be too sensitive to such atmosphere, he would be unfit for the office he held. He subdued a momentary inclination to defer the subject upon his mind, till he should be able to speak to Lady Denton alone, as he reflected that Gerard was inferior to herself both in discretion and self-control, and that his reaction to the conversation might possibly be the more illuminating of the two.

"I wonder," he said, addressing himself directly to Lady Denton, after one of the longer pauses between the efforts of conversation which she would make, and which had quickly died, like a plant in a shallow soil, "whether you could give me any further help as to what Mr. Redwin may have in mind. He has given me a rather insolent assurance that if I cannot discover who is responsible for Sir Daniel's death by next Monday afternoon, he will give information at that time which will enable me to do so."

Watching narrowly as he said this, he observed no more than that Gerard Denton's face assumed the look of stubborn sulkiness which was his habitual attitude toward the subject of his brother's death. His eyes fell to his plate. He thought, but was less than sure, that Lady Denton became slightly paler as he mentioned the late secretary's name. Her brows met in a little frown, though she puzzled over the problem he had put before her. In the moment's pause before she replied, he added, "I've no idea what it can be, and he's not a man whose word I should take for sixpence unless it were supported in other ways, but it's interesting that he should profess that he can solve the problem."

"It would he a great relief if he could," Lady Denton replied, "but I can't say I'm very hopeful of anything coming from him. I don't see how he could. He's not likely to say he had anything to do with it himself. It's most likely to be no more than a theory he's worked out in his own mind, and—well, the kind of theory that would be likely from such a man."

"You mean it would be malicious?"

"I think you can be quite sure about that. It's about the only thing you could be sure of in anything coming from that direction. I should say that he would try to make out that I murdered my husband myself, if he thought he could get anyone to believe such an improbable tale."

Her voice, as she said this, was cool and level, and her eyes met his in an open way, but yet he had the impression that she sometimes gave that she was not speaking without reserve. Rather, that it was with a cool deliberate boldness that she outfaced an accusation that she would rather speak with her own lips than have whispered behind her back.

He thought also that Gerard experienced some emotion, whether of wonder or consternation, which he controlled with difficulty as he heard her, but this was of an uncertain significance.

Beyond that, he felt that his actual question had not been very explicitly answered, and he added: "I don't suppose you're far wrong about that. But, anyway, there's nothing of which you know to suggest what line he's likely to take?"

There was a second's pause, and then she answered, with the same clear deliberation as before: "No, there's nothing except that suggestion about the taxes that Mr. Wheeler told you before. And that's almost too silly for words. But you never know with a man like he is."

"Well," the Inspector concluded, "I must just wait, and hear what he's got to say. I dare say it won't be much." He added, with an evident sincerity, and to the satisfaction of those who heard: "I'd give something to put that man in his proper place." And his tone left no doubt of where it would be likely to be.

He felt that he had said all he could, and to no great result, in which he was widely wrong, and he let a subject drop which neither of his table companions showed any disposition to keep alive. He mentioned casually that he would be out during the afternoon, having resolved to give Mr. Fisher a call, on the theory that a good huntsman should not abandon the chase because the game is scarce or the scent poor. He gained nothing by that call, beyond the information that Mr. Wheeler had kept his word, and Lady Denton's money—to the amount of £15,000—had been advanced to the support of her late husband's account, and, as it were, in bold assertion that he had neither died by his own hand, nor been murdered by her.

But Lady Denton, stretched in apparent idleness on her couch, with the excuse of headache for the quiet of a darkened room, was using her brains to a more momentous and immediate issue. She got up to refresh herself with tea at the usual hour, and then wrote a short note, which she subsequently motored to Wickfield to post there with her own hand, and returned in a recovered quietude of mind for the evening meal.

It was a serenity which had been shaken at lunchtime to an extent which it had been very hard to control, for at that time the vague fears of the last two days had come to a definite head, as the Inspector mentioned the promise—or threat—to her that Redwin had made. She had been forced by his final question to a denial which, she saw, would be subject to very adverse interpretation if the truth—or even as much of the truth regarding those letters as she had thought it wise to confide to Mr. Wheeler's sympathetic ears—should be disclosed in a hostile way.

Yet with an instant only for decision, and with Gerard hearing all that was said, denial, explicit and absolute, had seemed the safer, and almost the only, possible choice. She had relied—she might rely still—upon the difficulty that Redwin must find in any version of events which would involve her in a motive for the crime which was so near to being attributed to her, without inculpating himself to an almost equal criminality. She relied also, to a less extent, upon the difficulty he might have in proving any charge that he could contrive to make while keeping his own actions clean. But she found insufficient reassurance in that, for she was clear-minded enough to see that a mere theory of motive, falling far short of proof, might be enough to induce the issuing of the warrant which would place her in a criminal dock—might even make the final difference in the minds of a jury in whom reluctance to convict an attractive woman on evidence of so circumstantial a nature might be balanced precariously against the difficulty of postulating any other person who could have committed the crime.

But what was done was done. It was too late to alter, and of no avail to regret. She might have chosen badly or well, but she must now stake all on the denial that she had made. Only, she saw that Mr. Wheeler must know; and, vaguely, she felt some hope that he would not be slow or impotent to come to her aid. Finally she had written this note:

Dear Mr. Wheeler,

You will be interested to know that Mr. Redwin has promised to give Inspector Pinkey some information on Monday afternoon next which, if he is to be believed, will lead to the discovery of the cause of Sir Daniel's death.

You will judge whether, or in what way, he will be likely to keep his promise.

It will, of course, be a great relief if the matter can be cleared up, but I own I have little confidence in anything coming from such a source, or expectation that it can be based on anything better than his animosity toward those who discovered his dishonesty and caused his dismissal.

But you will judge these matters far better than I. I just thought that I ought to let you know what is happening here.

Sincerely,

Adelaide Denton

CHAPTER XXIII.

After all, it was the blindness of chance (or predestined fate) which played the decisive card, when it gave Mr. Wheeler occasion to look in at his office on Saturday morning, which it was not his habit to do. He glanced through some opened letters which had been placed on his desk in readiness for his Monday morning attention, and at two which had been left unopened, being marked "personal" on the envelopes. One of these he threw down as being well able to wait his leisure. The other, which bore the Wickfield postmark, and a crest on the flap which he knew well, he opened.

When he had done this, he sat down to think, and read the letter again. As he did so, he whistled to himself in an unprofessional manner, as he was too addicted to doing. He knew quite well how Sir Daniel had died, ever since he had asked Lady Denton a question about a drawer. He saw the peril in which she stood now.

He admired the coolness and address with which she faced the net of circumstances which had closed upon her. The letter itself—which told all he needed to know, and yet could do her no harm into whoever's hand it might fall—did it not make him wish that fate had led her to be on his own staff, rather than wasted her in idle affluence as Sir Daniel's wife? But without his aid, for which she so clearly appealed, he doubted whether the qualities he admired could be sufficient to save her now.

After a few minutes' thought, he rang for a clerk, and told him to ask Mr. Ashfield if he would kindly spare him a few minutes.

Mr. Ashfield was the firm's managing clerk, and, as often happens in such offices, had two-thirds of the responsibility and four-fifths of the work of the firm on his own shoulders.

Mr. Ashfield promptly came, and was met with Mr. Wheeler's customary geniality.

"Morning, Ashfield. Thought you'd be here. Wish you'd take a bit more time off than you do. Mr. Romer coming in today?"

"No, sir, he rarely does come in on Saturday morning now."

"Well, who does?" Mr. Wheeler was quite content that the instructions he was about to give should not come to the ears of the conveyancing partner, a man punctilious for the etiquette of the profession and all the usages of the law. "Bedford here?"

"Yes, sir, I think he is."

"Then send him to me. And I say, Ashfield: this goes no further. I want Bedford personally till Tuesday morning, perhaps more or less."

"Yes, sir, I understand." So he did. Bedford was to be employed in some way which would not appear in the firm's diary, or be set out in its bills of costs—and there was not the least occasion for Mr. Romer's mind to be worried as to what it might be.

A moment later Bedford came into the room. Picked up on a race course, where he had done Mr. Wheeler a valuable and unlooked-for service, he was a small, plump, middle-aged man with a good-humoured expression, but weasel's eyes. He had been with the firm for over four years now as enquiry agent, process server, and for any business, generally of an outside character, requiring shrewdness or observation. There seemed to be little of the ways or haunts or personalities of the criminal world that he did not know.

"Bedford," Mr. Wheeler said, "I hope your wife isn't expecting you home tonight."

"No, sir, not particular, sir."

No one knew whether Bedford had a wife, or a home, or, indeed, anything about his private affairs. He opposed a cheerful blankness to any personal question. What he was instructed to do he did cheerfully and efficiently, and those things were sometimes of a rather surprising kind. What he was paid he took in the same spirit, and on that score he had no reason for complaint, for the business that went through Mr. Wheeler's office was often of very remunerative kinds, and good service was rewarded with a wide-open hand.

"That," Mr. Wheeler replied, "is a good thing for her. I want you to do a little job for me at Beacon's Cross. I dare say it will take you the weekend, but I don't know, and I shan't ask, so long as it gets done.

"There's a man there, staying at the Station Inn. His name's Redwin. He's a thief and a blackmailer, and I dare say a few other things of the same kind. But that doesn't concern us. You'd better not know anything more about him before you arrive, and then you'll learn what you do in a natural way. I don't mean that any harm's to come to him. I needn't say that to you. But he's not to be there on Monday. He's to be 'gone, no address,' and if he leaves his hotel bill unpaid, I shan't blame you for that. But he's got to go, and I never want to know how."

"No, sir, you wouldn't want to know that. Is it a case where I can spend what I think best?"

"Money," Mr. Wheeler answered deliberately, "doesn't matter at all. But I don't know that you'll find it the right way. I shouldn't say he's a poor man."

"Would a dying mother be any good, sir?"

"No, I shouldn't say he's that sort. And besides, I don't want him back on the next day."

"No, sir. I see, sir. I'd better look up the trains."

"You won't fail to do this?"

"No, sir, of course not, sir."

Mr. Wheeler went to his private safe. He counted out ten ten-pound notes.

"These," he said, "are for yourself. They are not, of course, to be used in the case. What you have to spend will be in pound notes. I don't need to say that."

"No, sir, you don't need to say that."

"Have you got enough of your own?"

"Yes, sir, thank you, sir. I'll let you know what I spend when I get back."

Bedford went to consult the timetable, and Mr. Wheeler, after reading Lady Denton's letter again, put a match to a laid fire in the grate and used it to assist in kindling the wood. The envelope went the same way. He departed to his weekend golf with an easy mind, and the consciousness that a good deed had been put in hand.

Two hours later Mr. Bedford alighted from a third-class carriage at Beacon's Cross Station, and with a cheerful and yet thoughtful countenance, strolled round the district until the hour of opening enabled him to enter the Silver Trout, which is a small but quite respectable public house almost opposite to the Station Inn.

He sat there during the evening hours, absorbing as much gossip and as little beer as the circumstances allowed, and then went to put up for the night at the Station Inn.

As the hours of the evening passed he had learnt much of the local gossip, including some facts about Mr. Redwin and the occupants of Bywater Grange which Inspector Pinkey was never likely to hear, and had formed a (quite erroneous) theory of why Mr. Wheeler desired to rid the district so promptly of the ex-secretary's presence. He developed at least three excellent plans for securing that result during the night, which are best unmentioned, lest this narrative should reach the hands of those who might use them to more mischievous ends. And in the morning he descended to make the acquaintance of his destined victim, and saw, at the first glance, that he had been wasting his time, for this was a case where his subtler ingenuities would not be needed.

He stood at the door of the breakfast room, at the table of which Mr. Redwin was seated. Redwin was aware that someone had entered, but did not trouble to turn his head. He was in no mood to encourage strangers to conversation, being one of those who wake with an evil mind, even though it may mellow somewhat in the later hours of the day; and he was vexed that Monday was now drawing so near, while he had still been unable to devise a plan which would be decisive for Lady Denton's undoing without landing him in the witness box, if not the dock. Very different places in themselves, but which, he knew, might prove to be singularly alike to him.

He was just putting the last rasher of bacon on to his plate, and considering the difficulties of his position with a scowling countenance, when a voice at his elbow said, in the language of politeness as it is practised in a Bloomsbury lodging house: "After you with the salt."

He passed the salt cellar mechanically to the man who had sat down beside him, and as he did so recognition came to his eyes. He stared a moment at Mr. Bedford in an obvious consternation, and then controlled himself to say, with an outward aspect of geniality: "Hullo, Rogers. Where have you sprung from?"

"Hullo, Timothy," Bedford responded, with a cordiality which was less difficult but equally insincere. "Same to you."

"Don't call me that," Mr. Redwin protested in an anxious undertone. "I've not used that name for five years. Redwin's my name now."

"Mr. Redwin," Bedford replied, with a slight accent on the name, in which he appeared to find some humour which a listener might have been unable to share, "I'll give you an hour to clear out before I tell the police."

Redwin went pale at the threat, though he thought it to be no more than a matter of settling the price which would leave him free. "I don't see," he said, "what good you'd get out of that. What about fifty quid?"

Mr. Bedford's expression was one of undisturbed good humour as he replied: "I'll give you half an hour to get out of here before I tell the police."

"What about two fifties?"

Mr. Bedford seemed to enjoy the conversation more than ever. "I'll give you ten minutes," he said, "to clear out before I phone the police."

Mr. Redwin stared in a bewildered and frightened silence, not daring another bid in a form of auction at which he was losing so rapidly. Did the man mean what he said? They looked at each other, and a measure of understanding must have entered Mr. Redwin's mind. The execution of a warrant for embezzlement, issued against him in the name of Timothy Forsyth, which he had successfully evaded for five difficult but not unprosperous years, was not to be lightly risked, even for Lady Denton's undoing. He saw that it might be something more than a casual coincidence which had brought the one-time bookmaker's tout to his elbow now. He dared not speak again, lest the allotted time should be further reduced. He gulped down his coffee and got up to go. Five minutes later he strolled out of the inn, hoping, as he did so, that the proprietor would notice nothing singular in the fact that he should go out on Sunday morning carrying a suitcase that showed evidence of having been closed with difficulty. His exit was unobserved and unobstructed, and after walking a short distance along the London road, he stopped a coach which put him down at Oxford Circus in time for an early lunch.

Mr. Bedford paid his bill, feeling that there was no reason to incur the expense of a second night. He wondered how soon the proprietor would become aware that Mr. Redwin's account was not destined to be balanced in the same way. But (he reflected with satisfaction) the man had probably left enough luggage to straighten that out.

CHAPTER XXIV.

Having observed the exit of Mr. Redwin, it is necessary to return to the events of Friday, when Adelaide Denton had been writing to Mr. Wheeler, while the Inspector was returning to the police station from the offices of Forbes and Fisher.

On arriving there he, had called up Scotland Yard, and the result of a few minutes' conversation was such that he decided to return to headquarters immediately.

He sent a messenger to Bywater Grange to collect his suitcase, and with a brief note to Lady Denton to say that he had to go up to London, but expected to return on Monday.

Lady Denton, who thought that she had overcome his unwillingness to remain longer at the Grange (as, at the moment, she had), was surprised and not entirely pleased when she read this, for she was one who would rather be in contact with any danger that might beset her than that it should be withdrawn from sight while its existence continued. She saw also that there was a possible menace, either to herself or her brother-in-law, in this withdrawal; for the Inspector might dislike the idea of remaining a guest in the house, if he were now occupied definitely in completing the evidence which would enable him to advise the arrest of one of its inmates.

To Gerard Denton, however, the news had a better sound, for it was the loathed presence of the Inspector which broke his nerves, and made the overhanging shadow blacker and more imminent than it would otherwise have been. Even the ordeal that was before him on Monday evening receded somewhat, and seemed less formidable, as he realized that he could come to meals without the hated presence of that red-headed policeman appearing opposite to spoil the flavour of all he ate.

The decision which the Inspector had made may have been influenced by a natural reluctance to strain further the hospitality of a house which, as he was increasingly persuaded in his own mind, must contain the murderer whom it was his duty to run to earth, but this was certainly not the decisive consideration, and he would have put his own feelings, and even what some might consider to be the elementary decencies of human conduct, finally aside had he thought that his immediate object would have been advanced by a longer residence there.

But the fact was that he had come to a point at which he was disposed to report the difficulty of the position to his superiors, and to take counsel with, and instructions from them, rather than the undivided responsibility either of advising that Superintendent Trackfield had been right in his intention of arresting Lady Denton, in which case the warrant would at once have been issued, or that Gerard Denton were the more probable culprit, on which it was almost equally certain that his arrest would promptly follow.

Without entirely dismissing the possibilities either of suicide, or of an unnamed and unsuspected criminal, he yet considered the difficulties of those solutions to be so great, and the circumstantial evidence against Gerard and Lady Denton so strong, that he would probably have advised the arrest of either but for the presence of the other upon the scene, or in the neighbourhood of the crime.

As an abstract proposition, he saw that the suspicion against the wife of the murdered man was, in some aspects, the simpler, stronger case, and would have been decidedly so had he been able to discover any adequate motive, or even develop a plausible theory as to what motive there might have been.

And when the question of motives engaged his mind, the scale would tilt in a provoking manner, for, if Gerard were innocent, what adequate reason had he for the way in which he had bribed the boy? And did not the very fact that he could still consider the possibility of Gerard being the actual murderer—and of the boy and him being now in the conspiracy of a common lie—show that the case against Lady Denton was less than proved, even to the logic of his own mind? Or was it only that he was subconsciously influenced by the fact that Lady Denton was an attractive woman, and Gerard Denton a most unattractive man?

But one thing was plain. For him to advise an arrest which should afterwards appear to have been a mistake, would be a blot on his reputation which ten years of subsequent successes would not entirely remove, and which would be unforgotten until the day when he should retire, and beyond that. It might be the single incident by which his name would continue in the memory of the Yard. The reflection led him, by a widely different path, to Mr. Wheeler's conclusion, that it was a case which could best be left to the irresponsible guessing of a coroner's jury, men who could wrangle and differ, and perhaps decide at last by the chance of a spun coin, in the seclusion of their own room, and depart namelessly, without concern for the consequences their verdict bore.

But in any event the sole responsibility must not be his. He must report in such a way that he would be able to throw the responsibility as far as possible upon his superiors, and in such a form that it could not afterwards be said that he had failed to present any factor of the problem, the importance of which he should have appreciated while on the spot.

With these thoughts in his mind, supported by the fact that he had no evident line of further enquiry to follow, until the time should come for that distasteful appointment with Redwin on Monday afternoon, and with a natural inclination to spend the weekend at Balham with a waiting wife, even the natural repugnance which he felt to remaining in a house where he was so clearly unwelcome may have been no more than a subordinate factor in the resolution that he had formed.

Yet while the train ran Londonward, down the gradients of the Chiltern Hills, he was conscious of recovered freedom as he thought that he might have passed the gates of Bywater Grange for the last time, and of relief, as of one who opens a window to fresher air.

He came back by an early train on Monday morning with a renewed confidence, having had his conduct of the investigation approved and his opinions confirmed. The fact that he had discovered the bribery of the gardener's boy, and the deliberate omission in the statements which he and Gerard Denton had made, was sufficient to support the prestige of the Yard as against that of the rural constabulary; and he now had definite instructions to avoid the risk of a more radical error on his own side, by declining to advise an arrest, unless he should make some further discovery of a vital value. He was to take amended statements from both Gerard Denton and Tommy, and to examine carefully any evidence or theory that Redwin might put before him; but, unless he should then find that he had to deal with a radically different situation, he was to advise that the coroner should be notified by Superintendent Trackfield that the police had no intention of making an arrest on the information they already had, and that the adjourned inquest could therefore be held without more delay.

Such an inquest would not only relieve the police of a difficult decision, it would have the advantage of requiring those who had been in the neighbourhood of the tragedy, other than directly suspected persons, to be further examined, publicly and on oath; and even those on whom suspicion might clearly lie could be invited to

113

give such evidence, after being warned that they were not bound to incriminate themselves—and how often can a person who professes innocence afford to avail himself of so insidious a relief?

He went at once to the police station and asked: "Any news?" when he met Superintendent Trackfield, without expectation of an affirmative reply.

"No. I can't say there's much. Or not what looks that way to me. I saw Lady Denton at church yesterday. Charming as ever, and seems to be getting a good deal of sympathy. Gerard Denton—I've had a discreet watch kept upon him—went for a walk in the afternoon on the Loudwater road, and Briggs tells me that Bulger's preached a very vigorous sermon on minding your own business, and believing less than you hear rather than more.

"There's a possible importance in the fact that Redwin hasn't been seen since yesterday morning, and there's a report that he got onto a London coach. I'm not sure that I ought not to have put someone on his track, but we've nothing against him officially, whatever we may believe him to be; and it's seemed that nothing would drive him away, rather than that there should be any difficulty in keeping him here."

"Did he tell them he was going? I mean at the inn."

"No. They didn't know till they noticed he wasn't making his meals. And they're sure he didn't come in at night."

"Luggage gone?"

"No—or, at least, not the bulk."

"Then you can be sure he'll be back. It rather looks as though he's gone off to get some evidence to put before us this afternoon. It would account for fixing it for today."

"Yes, there's something in that—"

"I've been talking things over at the Yard, and we don't see that there's a sufficiently certain case against either Gerard or Lady Denton to advise an arrest, if we can't get a bit more evidence than we have now. It seems likely enough that it was one of the two, but the question is which. It's not as though they'd been doing burglary or any other illegal act, so that you could say it was between the two, and you didn't need to go deeper than that. Of course, it may have been that the two were in collusion, but we want more evidence, or more theory of motive, than we have to sustain that. And if they had been, wouldn't they have put up a better tale?"

"I've always thought," the Superintendent replied, "that the murder wasn't deliberate, whoever did it. They wouldn't have done it like that, with the boy weeding the drive outside. And that rather sits on the idea of collusion between the two."

"Perhaps it does, but if it wasn't deliberate, what was it, when he was shot from behind with a gun taken out of his own drawer?"

"Anyway, you don't advise an arrest?"

"Not off your own bat. Let the coroner get to work, and his jury'll hold the baby more likely than not. That's unless we get something worthwhile from Redwin this afternoon. But we're to get Gerard Denton's and the boy's statements revised, and that reminds me to ring him up and make sure he'll be coming in."

He called up Bywater Grange, asking to speak to Mr. Denton, but it was Lady Denton who answered the phone.

"Yes," she said, "is it anything I can do? He's not down yet. He's not very well."

"It was only to remind him that we are expecting him here at seven tonight, to get his statement a bit nearer to the facts as we have them now."

"Would an earlier hour be equally convenient?"

"No, I'm afraid it wouldn't. I've got another appointment this afternoon, and I don't know how long it will take."

"Oh yes, of course. I'd forgotten that. I'll remind him when he comes down."

"Thank you, Lady Denton. In his own interest, if I may speak plainly—"

"Yes, I quite understand. You can depend on his being there."

She rang off rather promptly at that, as though not wishing the conversation to be further prolonged.

"I should think," Inspector Pinkey said thoughtfully, "she's having a bit of trouble with that bounder. But she'll have him here to time. There's not much doubt about that. I don't know which of them shot Sir Daniel—I wish I did—but there's no doubt of who's got the brains at Bywater Grange."

Lady Denton did have some difficulty with her brother-in-law. He came down to lunch, and when she told him of the telephone conversation he said moodily that he didn't see why he should go, and he didn't think that he would.

The fact was that the Inspector's absence since Friday had enabled Gerard Denton to put some particularly unpleasant thoughts more or less out of his mind, and he was very unwilling to permit their re-entrance. He had gone through life with a habit of evasion which had so far succeeded, at whatever negation of self-discipline, in avoiding most of the acuter troubles and discomforts which are the common experience of those who play the game in a manlier way.

Lady Denton's delicate lip lifted slightly in contempt, as she answered: "You'd be an utter fool if you didn't go. If you do, you've got nothing to fear. But, if you don't, it's like accusing yourself."

"I don't see that I've got nothing to fear. I think I'm in a rotten hole, and if I go, I don't know what they'll get me to say."

"You've only got to tell the truth. That ought to be easy enough, even for you."

"Tell the truth?" Gerard Denton stared at her. "You don't really want me to do that?"

There was a moment's silence between the two, and then Lady Denton answered coolly: "You know perfectly well what I mean. You haven't got to say anything that they wouldn't believe, and you needn't make it look worse for me than the facts are that we can't help, though it seems to me that you did that from the first, whether you meant it or not. You've only got to say what Tommy's told them already, and they won't get him to change. I've had a word with him myself about that."

"Yes, it's easy for you to talk, but suppose they do get him to say something different? You don't see that it's worse for me than for you. They don't hang women. It'd be fifteen years at the worst. I don't see—"

His voice died away before the fury of anger in Lady Denton's eyes.

"Are you proposing," she asked, "that I should spend fifteen years in a filthy gaol because you...." She checked herself abruptly, and ended: "...haven't the courage, or nerve, or common sense of...." The sentence was unfinished again. She had regained her self-control when she said coldly: "If you don't mind, Gerard, we won't talk about this any more. There are times when you make me a little sick."

And after that there was silence between the two.

CHAPTER XXV.

Inspector Pinkey went to the Station Inn to meet Mr. Redwin in the afternoon, having decided upon the firm and even minatory attitude with which he would uphold the dignity of the law (and that of the police force of the metropolis). He had several sentences already framed in his mind with which any unseemly levity or truculence could be abashed. Should the man continue to hint at things which he would not say, he would warn him that a very unpleasant time might be before him in the witness box at the coming inquest. He had formulated some excellent plans of assault upon Mr. Redwin's reticence, and was not without hope that he might be about to add another to the more conspicuous successes of his career. But, as it has been easy to anticipate, they remained untested, for the sufficient reason that Mr. Redwin was not there. He was represented by a rather large trunk, and a disorderly scattering of some articles suggestive of the departure of a man who had packed in haste.

After the Inspector had waited an hour, the landlord showed him this room, which he considered carefully, with a strong and natural desire to subject Mr. Redwin's effects to the expert examination which he was well qualified to make; but on considering that the man, in leaving his room for the weekend, had committed no offence known to the criminal law, and that if, at any moment he should return and find the Inspector kneeling beside a half-emptied trunk, it might be a discordant prelude to the intended interview, he reluctantly deferred a pleasure which he was to experience on a later day.

He waited two hours longer, knocking the balls about on the table of a deserted billiard room, and then went back reluctantly to the police station, having arranged with the landlord to ring him up in the event of Mr. Redwin's return.

It seemed that he must have the interview with Gerard Denton without the advantage of whatever revelations Mr. Redwin would have been able to make, but in this anticipation he was wrong again, for seven o'clock came and went, but Mr. Denton did not.

Inspector Pinkey sat with Superintendent Trackfield waiting for him to arrive, and at four minutes after seven he made his customary remark for such occasions that they were generally a little late, but not much. At seven-twenty he was definitely uneasy, and at seven-twenty-five he felt that he might have been too emphatic when he had rejected the Superintendent's suggestion that they should phone Bywater Grange ten minutes before, on the ground that it would be a mistake to show anxiety on their side.

He remembered Lady Denton's remark that morning that Gerard was upstairs, and unwell, to which he had attached little importance at the time. He knew that the gentleman was addicted to spending the earlier half of his mornings on the upper floor, and it had seemed a very natural condition for him to be in. But, at the same time, he had had her assurance that Gerard would not fail to come, and he had a strong conviction that, had he been prevented by subsequent illness, she would have made some communication to that effect.

"I'll tell you what, Trackfield," he said, "we won't phone. If we do, we may just be put off with a tale that he isn't well, and we shan't know whether it's true or false. We'll just take a run up to the house. We'll get nearer the truth, and it'll be a lesson to him that he can't treat us just how he likes. And if he thinks we've come to run him in, when he hears there are two of us at the door—well, there mayn't be much harm in that."

It was in a mood to stand no nonsense from anybody that he got out of the car and rang the bell rather sharply at Bywater Grange; for his patience had been strained more than sufficiently during the long wait of the afternoon, and he had a well-founded instinct that things had been happening around him which were outside his knowledge, and which it was his business to understand. He was vexed by an uneasy fear that Redwin might have made the appointment with no intention of keeping it, nor of giving him information at any time, but only to hold him back from decisive action for a period required for some purpose which he was unable to guess. No one likes to be fooled, and it is particularly provoking to those whose living and reputation depend upon their ability to interpret the facts around them.

It seemed likely that Gerard Denton was to suffer as a result of Mr. Wheeler's successful strategy, which that gentleman certainly had not foreseen or intended, and which may be held to demonstrate how unforeseeable the results of the most astute of human actions may be. Or, at least, it might have been held to demonstrate it, only that it didn't turn out in that way. With no unusual delay, Pauline opened the door.

She looked somewhat surprised when asked if Mr. Gerard Denton were in, and a little alarmed, which the sight of the two officers may have been sufficient to explain. But she did not answer, for she had left the door of the dining room open, having been serving there when the bell rang, and Lady Denton heard Inspector Pinkey's voice in the hall.

She called out: "Pauline, show the gentlemen in here." She rose to meet them, seeming a little surprised, even a little agitated, at this untimely invasion. But she asked them courteously if they would join her at the meal.

They said no to that. Could they see Mr. Denton? Was he not in?

"I think there must have been a misunderstanding," she replied. "He told me he was seeing you at the police station this evening. That was what was arranged."

"Yes, but he didn't come."

"He's not usually very punctual. I expect you'll find he's there now."

"Could you say how long it is since he left the house?"

"He hasn't been in since just after tea. At least, I think not. He asked me to walk with him, as he'd got something to tell me, so I went a little way and then turned back. I understood that he was staying out till it was time for his appointment with you. But it wasn't clear. He seemed rather upset."

"Which way did he go?"

"We went a little way up the Highcombe Road—the old road—the one that goes over the hill."

Inspector Pinkey looked enquiry at his companion. He knew little of the local roads.

"He might have gone over the hill and come back through Loudwater. It wouldn't take much over the hour at a steady pace."

They went back to the police station, but Gerard Denton was not there.

CHAPTER XXVI.

At a later hour, when Lady Denton received the two police offi-cers at Bywater Grange, they said that there could be no doubt that, if Gerard Denton had not returned home, he must have fled in pref-erence to facing further enquiry, and they asked for additional in-formation as to the circumstances in which he had left the house. They required also to question the servants as to whether he might have returned without Lady Denton's knowledge. They had already sent out urgent instructions to the police over a sufficient area to de-tain anyone answering his description who should be unable to es-tablish a separate identity.

"It's a queer thing," Lady Denton said, "and I scarcely know what to think. But I can't believe that he's run away, as you seem to suppose. It's not like Gerard somehow, even if there'd been more cause than there is. He's—he's not got the pluck, if you understand what I mean. And beside that, he'd got nothing with him. And no money, so far as I know. He couldn't have had very much. Yes, you can ask the servants, of course. He might have come in again with-out telling me. But he isn't in his own room. We've looked there more than once already."

Inspector Pinkey said: "Well, we'd better see round while we're here, but I don't suppose he'll have come back."

"You can go anywhere that you wish," Lady Denton replied. "I dare say Pauline could show you round, unless you want me."

They agreed that Pauline would be a satisfactory guide, and a thorough search assured them that Gerard Denton was not there, unless he were hiding in the outbuildings, which was not a probable supposition, and which it was too dark to decide with certainty.

They went back to the drawing room, where Lady Denton had considerately ordered that coffee should be brought in (she already knew that Inspector Pinkey was not addicted to any more potent stimulant), and reported their non-success.

120

"I can't say I'm surprised," the Inspector said, "after Redwin clearing off in the same way." He looked closely at Lady Denton as he said this, and was satisfied that she, at least, was not previously aware of that circumstance. She looked surprised, and, he thought more doubtfully, relieved, as though he had given her welcome and unlooked-for news. But perhaps it was natural that she should take it in that way, for Redwin had surely been of no friendship to her.

"You mean," she asked, "that Mr. Redwin has left Beacon's Cross?"

"Yes, he walked out of the Station Inn yesterday morning, leaving most of his luggage behind, and hasn't been seen since."

"And you think that that has some connection with the way that Gerard's gone now? Then I must say that I'm sure you're wrong. They hated each other, for one thing; and, in any case, they'd no reason to go off together. It isn't sense that they should."

The Inspector felt again that Lady Denton spoke with sincerity, and it inclined him to exculpate her from any responsibility for the double flight, as he believed it to be. He was in better spirits than he had been earlier in the day, for he felt that the criminals had gone far to resolve his problem by the folly of their own actions. It was almost an admission of common guilt. Perhaps Redwin had been planning to mislead him this afternoon with some lying tale, probably to turn suspicion in Lady Denton's direction, and it had since been decided between the actual culprits that it was too dangerous an attempt. Possibly the scale had been turned when he had discovered the bribery of the gardener's boy. And so they had preferred to fly—to fly separately, to confuse suspicion and make pursuit more difficult.

It looked now as though the murder had been the fruit of a common plot—probably of Redwin's design, although Gerard's had been the hand which had fired the shot. And he had done it in a blundering way, and at a foolish time, with the boy outside on the drive, which were just the kind of mistakes that Gerard Denton would be likely to make. Doubtless, suicide was to have been the apparent fact—suicide, with the explanation that Sir Daniel had been worried over his taxation irregularities, and a threatened exposure intolerable to one of his sensitive pride.

It was a theory in which the Inspector was fundamentally wrong on more than one point, as it is easy to see, but he had not had the advantage of overhearing the conversation between Bedford and Redwin at the dining table of the Station Inn, and the most expert mathematician cannot be expected to add a column correctly, if only one of its figures be concealed from view.

The Inspector's judgment, after a week of indecision, came, though somewhat late, to the definite conclusion that Lady Denton had no part in the crime. Her tale, he considered, simple and straightforward from the first, of how she had run into the study at the sound of the shot and her husband's fall, had been neither more nor less than the truth, as such unshaken statements most often are.

He knew that she had no strength of affection for her brother-in-law, who was not of a type, either physically or mentally, to which such a woman as she appeared to be would be likely to give more than the toleration that the relationship required; and his conviction that she was an innocent party to the tragedy led him to appeal to her now, with a new confidence, for any help that she might be able to give.

"I wonder," he asked, "whether you can recall anything that was said during the day that would throw any light on his state of mind, or probable movements after you parted. You say he asked you to walk some distance with him. That, in itself, was rather unusual, wasn't it?"

"Yes, perhaps it was. But it didn't seem so at the time. He's been very moody all day; and he was very unwilling to come to see you this evening. He made no secret of that. Indeed, we were discussing it all through lunch, till I got fed up and told him he'd better stop.

"I suppose it was you having found out that he'd given Tommy the pound note that he couldn't get out of his mind."

"You had known about that all along?"

"Yes, he told me the next day, and I said then that I thought it was a mad thing to have done. I told him that such things always come out in the end, and then look worse than they are."

"What reason did he give you for having done it?"

"Just the same as he does now. He didn't want it to come out that he'd left Sir Daniel just before he was shot, or of the row that they'd had then."

"He made no secret about the row?"

"No, he couldn't have done that. I overheard part of it, if not all."

"Was it exceptionally violent?"

"No, just ordinary. Nothing more than they often had."

"Did he give any reason for asking you to go out with him to-night?"

"No, not exactly. I thought he wanted some encouragement or advice about seeing you. I'd shut him up rather sharply at lunch-time, so it wasn't as surprising as it may sound."

"Did you go far?"

"Yes, I think it was about the bend of the road, where it goes over the hill. I didn't notice particularly. I'd said I'd turn back more than once, when I understood he was staying out, and then he'd start talking again."

"What about?"

"About seeing you tonight, and the mess he'd be in if you got Tommy to say anything that wasn't true. It was all about that."

"About something that wasn't true? Or perhaps something that was?"

"No. He said Tommy was telling the truth now, and I said I believed he was, and, if so, I couldn't see what he'd got to fear. He said he'd have a stroll round till it was time to see you, as he didn't feel like coming in."

"And you thought he meant what he said?"

"Yes. And I do now. I suppose we shall know who's right in the end, but I don't think he had any intention of going away. I think he'd have behaved differently if he had."

Inspector Pinkey was not uninfluenced by this opinion, which had an echo in his own mind, but he had long learned the first lesson of successful detection, that both theories and opinions must give way to facts. "Still," he said, "there's the fact that he's not here."

"Yes," she agreed, and then: "Of course, he may have got into a panic and gone off in a silly way. It's the kind of thing he'd be rather likely to do. I mean, it's the way he'd do it, if he did it at all."

"Yes, I dare say it is. Lady Denton," he said very seriously, "I want to ask you a question to which I think there can be only one reply. Should you wish to shelter your husband's murderer in any circumstances, or whoever he might be?"

"No," she answered. "Certainly not. I suppose nobody would."

"Then I must ask this. In your own heart, can you acquit Mr. Gerard Denton of complicity in the crime?"

There was a pause of silence. Then she said, with a slow deliberation: "Yes, I see how it looks to you, and I suppose it will come out in the end, as things mostly do. But I don't think there was a crime at all. I think Daniel shot himself, though I don't profess to know why. But that's what I think, and that's what I shall always say."

"Well, Lady Denton, you won't get many people to agree with you about that."

"Which," she said, with a slight smile relieving the gravity of her face, "won't prove that I'm wrong."

CHAPTER XXVII.

Inspector Pinkey's rather extensive experience had shown him that the investigation of a crime such as that with which he was now dealing (if crime it were) would commonly pass through three phases. There would be, first, the hopeful stage when the preliminary evidence would be crowding in, and it would appear to be a brief and easy matter to prepare a convincing case against the most evident culprit. After that, there would frequently be a period of reaction and doubt, when other facts would appear which declined to fall in with the simplicity of the first hypothesis, and the baffled investigation would move round in widening circles, like a homing pigeon cast loose in a foreign land, flying round at greater heights till it perceives some distant landmark, and strikes straight and fast for the goal of its certain home.

It was this third stage that the Inspector supposed that he had now reached. He had little doubt that, if he could catch the two fugitives, the separate police examinations to which they would then be subjected would lead, if only by their discrepancies and denials, to the ultimate discovery of the truth, and the expiation of a deliberate and treacherous crime.

In the case of Gerard Denton, he felt that his proximity to the scene of the tragedy, and the fact that he was known to be on bad terms with his half-brother, joined to the bribery of the boy, and the falsehood of the signed statement which he had previously made, gave a significance to his flight which justified the issuing of an immediate warrant for his apprehension. Nor did he think that that event would be long delayed, when he considered his inexperience in evading capture, and the circumstances under which he had left his home.

In the case of Redwin, however significant the simultaneous disappearances might be to his own mind, he saw that he must proceed with greater caution. He had really nothing beyond the way in which he had been dismissed, his subsequent conduct, and his general character, to connect him with the crime, and he knew that no jury would convict, nor could he hope even to obtain his committal, without something of a much more definite character.

For the moment, he must be content to trace him, and then— well, a short "detained for enquiries," with all its attendant possibilities, would be clearly indicated.

And, of course, Gerard Denton might have been induced to speak before then, and supplied the necessary data on which to proceed against his companion in crime.

With these thoughts in a very confident mind, he obtained a warrant for Gerard Denton's arrest, and then decided to return to London, from which centre he could best direct the pursuit of the fugitives, while it would also enable him to resume duties which had been laid aside at the call of the present investigation.

Before doing this, he had a further talk with Lady Denton, and examined the other inmates of Bywater Grange regarding the behaviour of Gerard Denton before leaving the house; but he obtained nothing beyond a general confirmation of the account she had given, and a specific memory of the parlour maid, who had overheard part of Gerard's conversation with Lady Denton when he had asked her to go out, which supported her own account of that incident.

It was on the afternoon of Thursday, three days after Gerard Denton had disappeared, that the rigour of the search which had been instituted bore its expected fruit, in what, to continue the metaphor, may be described as a double crop; for Inspector Pinkey, coming in after an absence of several hours upon business with which we have no concern, was informed that Redwin had been run to earth in a Bermondsey lodging, where he had been living under an assumed name; and, before this had been fully assimilated, there was a phone call from Beacon's Cross with news of a kindred kind.

As to Redwin, it may be said that his fears were his own undoing. For when Detective Sprinkler called upon him with no more sinister purpose than to suggest that Redwin had been his surname for a longer period than the one that he now used, and to propose that he should come back to the station with him (which he would have had no power to enforce), he assumed too readily that his previous identity had been betrayed, which, until Mr. Bedford had sat down beside him on Sunday morning, he had regarded as securely buried.

Impulsed by this fear, his reply had been a sudden bolt for the door, on which Detective Sprinkler, a young but intelligent officer, considering that the less willing Mr. Redwin might be to enter a police station the more reason there might be that he should arrive at that destination, had tripped him up very adroitly, after which there had been a few minutes of very lively exchanges in which the bodies of both combatants took some bruises, and the furniture suffered more seriously. Finally, Mr. Redwin, accused of no crime, had the indignity of going to the police station with handcuffed wrists, and was promptly charged with the assault on Detective Sprinkler, not as an end in itself, but as a means of detaining him which he had himself been obliging enough to supply, while his capture could be reported to Scotland Yard, and his position in regard to the law receive the consideration that it deserved.

In view of the violent circumstances which had led to his reception, and the evident desirability of discovering as much as possible about him (particularly of an unsatisfactory character), the officer who took the charge, showing an intelligence equal to that of Detective Sprinkler, had also taken Mr. Redwin's fingerprints by one of those irregular methods which are only justified by their results, and by the time Inspector Pinkey came in, and received the news of his capture, it was accompanied by the interesting information that he had been identified as Timothy Pepworth Forsyth, who had served two earlier terms of imprisonment before he had disappeared, with a warrant for embezzlement issued against him.

Inspector Pinkey, having had no more than a single moment to digest this information, was called to the telephone to hear Superintendent Trackfield's voice at the other end of the wire.

"I thought," it said, "you'd like to know at once that Gerard Denton's been found."

"So's Redwin," he replied. "We seem to be having a good day. Where did you run him down?"

"We haven't exactly done that. He's dead."

"Suicide, I suppose?"

"I can't say that. We've no details as yet. Just the fact. But I thought I'd try to catch you before you left."

"Thanks for that." Inspector Pinkey thought quickly. Redwin, however much or little he might finally appear to have been concerned in the case, was in safe storage now. He would keep. He added: "I'll come down at once. There's a train, if I remember rightly—yes, in about half an hour. The fast evening train."

He heard Superintendent Trackfield's voice assuring him that he would meet him with his own car, and rang off.

CHAPTER XXVIII.

Gerard Denton had not been found by means of the elaborate network of espionage which had been spread for his snaring over some fifty thousand square miles of his native land. He had been found by a lurking poacher in a quarry pit, old and disused, which lay about three hundred yards aside from the Loudwater road. If Lady Denton's memory were correct that she had walked with him to the turn of the hill, he must have left the road almost immediately that they parted, to take the hedge-side path, now deserted and over-grown, that led to the fatal pit.

He lay among the rough stones of the quarry with a smashed arm and a broken neck. It was not a fall that any man could survive, nor was it one that could have come by accident in the dark. Not, at least, to one who knew the road, as he must have done. There was a closed gate to pass, and a walk along the quarry edge which was a mere track. It led nowhere.

It was dear that he had committed suicide, or had been mur-dered deliberately in that lonely spot; but against the latter hypothe-sis there was not only its inherent improbability—for who should have known that he would have been walking there, or could have compelled or lured him from the safer road, or could have sufficient motive for such a crime?—but at the place where he fell, which could be plainly seen by the broken gravel at the edge of the narrow path, there was no sign of a struggle that could be detected by the keen eyes of Inspector Pinkey, or of the Superintendent, who had accompanied him to the spot.

"It's just the chance of a dry season that we've found him at all," the Superintendent remarked. "He was lying half in the water and half out, as it was. Most years it would have been eight feet deep, if not more."

"Well," Inspector Pinkey replied, "it's just as well as it was. It made no difference to him, and it's saved us a lot of trouble, and probably some blame for having let him escape."

"It's not how I like a case to end, but it's better than if we'd had to leave it unsolved, or gone too far with something we couldn't prove, and got a slap in the face when the verdict came. He's made his statement now."

Superintendent Trackfield was not quick to reply. He saw the implication—which might not have been intended—against himself. Suppose he had carried out his own reluctant purpose of arresting Lady Denton for her husband's murder, where would he be now? Worse than that—for he saw that there were more issues than his own reputation which had been in the balance then—where would Lady Denton have been, and to what tragic blunder of justice might it not have led, when all the legal resources of the Crown would have been marshalled to prove her guilt?

He saw that he ought to put his own feelings aside in satisfaction that the case had been brought to a different end. But he would have been less than human had he failed also to see that its result would appear to justify the Chief Constable's decision to call in the assistance of Scotland Yard, with a corresponding disparagement of his own abilities. Well, suppose it were no more than the truth was? Suppose he were rather dull, or, at least, less sharp-witted than the brilliant lights of the metropolitan area? There were many stupid folk in the world who lost no sleep owing to their unalterable mental deficiency.

Probably, to the aloofness of archangelic minds, the mental difference between the greatest genius that the race of men had produced and its dullest boor was not enough to be easily recognized. And all the same (he thought rather obstinately), he should do the same again in the same position. As things were when the Chief Inspector came on the scene, he had thought the proper course was to apply for a warrant for Lady Denton's arrest. And that opinion he would not change, though he might be glad that things had turned out in a different way. For Lady Denton was an intelligent and attractive woman, and Gerard Denton a man who could be quite easily spared.

They walked back together to Bywater Grange, and saw Lady Denton there, who was grave enough, but did not express any deeper grief at her brother-in-law's tragic end than she had shown at her husband's death.

This was on the morning following Inspector Pinkey's return to Beacon's Cross, and Mr. Wheeler, whom she had summoned as soon as Gerard Denton's body had been discovered, arrived while they were there.

They met in the drawing room in Lady Denton's presence, and Mr. Wheeler, who had been considering the matter from several aspects as he journeyed down, said he was fortunate to have found them together. He didn't want to dictate in any way, but he supposed there would be no point now in deferring the inquest further—probably it would be convenient all round to hold both inquests on the same day?

"I own," he said, "that I shall be glad if you see no objection to that, and the Coroner looks at it in the same light, for I'm bound to be present at both, and just now I've got a rush of business from every side till I don't know what to leave, or to do first."

"I don't know that there'd be any objection from us," Inspector Pinkey said cautiously, "but it'll be for the Coroner to decide."

"Yes, of course, but I dare say you'll be able to let me know before I go back." And then to Lady Denton: "I'll stay to lunch, if I may?"

"Yes," she said; "I shall be glad if you will."

The two officers shortly left, and Lady Denton was alone with her solicitor.

"I suppose," she said, "you'll like to go over Gerard's papers. I'd rather leave them entirely to you, if I may. Mr. Trackfield had a look round last night, and a Mr. Leadbeater, from the Coroner's office, has been here for about two hours this morning—he only left half an hour ago—but I don't think they took anything away."

"I don't suppose they found anything sufficiently important to take," Mr. Wheeler replied easily, "and, in any case, they were within their rights if they did. They could only be interested in anything bearing on the causes of either death."

"They wouldn't be likely to find anything of that kind."

"No, not unless he had left a note."

"He wouldn't have done that. I don't believe Gerard had any idea of committing suicide. Not when he left the house."

Mr. Wheeler looked somewhat surprised at this statement, but he only said: "Well, you're in the best position to judge."

She frowned a little at this, as though puzzled by some possible implication it might contain, and then said in explanation: "Gerard never meant anything."

Mr. Wheeler recognized some profundity in this reflection. Whatever he might have done would be the result of the moment's impulse, the inadequacy of his own instincts of greed or fear to resist the impact of surrounding circumstance. It would be done from weakness rather than from strength of will; and if he had killed himself, it was most unlikely that it would have resulted from a settled purpose, such as would have left a letter behind him to announce the deed. Had he written such a letter, he would have been more likely, in a later vacillation of purpose, to have come back alive.

"No," he said, considering how singularly abortive Gerard Denton's life had been, either for evil or good, "I don't suppose there'll be much to interest me either. But I'd better have a look through. I don't think he had made a will."

Even his finances had been under the control of others. If it were a fact (which Mr. Wheeler did not believe) that he had murdered his brother to obtain possession of that which was his, it had been as abortive an act as might be expected from such a source. There could be no more of which to take control than the balance (if any) of the sum which had been lent by his own office a few days before, and the statement of any personal debts which might remain to be paid. It did not occur to him that Gerard Denton was the sort of man who might keep a diary very regularly and frankly entered.

Lady Denton led him to Gerard's room, and said: "You'll find a lot of old papers and books in the trunk in the clothes closet. That's where he turned up the pistol he had that was like Sir Daniel's. But Mr. Trackfield's been through them, and he says they're just old junk, of no value at all. The only places he left locked were the little desk in the window and the top drawer of the chest. They found the keys in his pocket, and after Mr. Leadbeater had gone over everything, he left them here."

She went away to the supervision of a house that she ordered well, and Mr. Wheeler turned to the investigation of the privacies of a dead client, as he had often had occasion to do before.

They met at lunch an hour later. He had brought down a small bundle of papers which he was taking away. "Apart from these," he said, "you can destroy anything which you regard as being of no value, so far as I am concerned. There are a few personal articles which must be valued for probate, but I needn't trouble you about them."

"It will be all right if I just tell Pauline that the papers can be destroyed?"

"Ye-es, I suppose it will, if you'd rather not do it yourself. There've been three of us over them now, and we seem agreed that there's nothing of value there. But you'd better not do that until after the inquest has been held."

"Mr. Leadbeater rang up a few minutes ago. He said the inquest will be held at eleven tomorrow morning, and the adjourned inquest at twelve. They're to be held at the Station Inn."

Mr. Wheeler considered these hours. There would be the visit to the mortuary, some distance away, to be got in, for the South Buckfordshire Coroner was of the old school, and still regarded the viewing of the body as an essential part of the ritual he controlled. There was a clear implication that the inquest on the body of Gerard Denton was not expected to be of a lengthy kind. He asked: "Same jury for both? I suppose he didn't say that?"

"No. He just told me the times and asked me to be sure to be there. He said a formal notice would follow, but he thought I should like to know first."

"Did you say I was here?"

"Yes, I said I would let you know."

"I must have a word with Pinkey before I leave, but I expect he'll be ringing up to give me the same information. I'll wait for that, if it doesn't keep me too long."

There was silence after that for some minutes. Lady Denton was not disposed for conversation of a wandering kind, and Mr. Wheeler's thoughts were concentrated upon the problem of how he could pass an idea from his mind to hers without the clumsiness of the spoken word.

"I suppose," he said at last, "you know that you'll be required to give evidence tomorrow morning?"

"Yes, I understood that."

"I don't mean that you've any need to worry. You're one of the best witnesses I ever heard. You answer clearly, and say just enough, and not a word more."

"I suppose it will be mainly about how Gerard left the house, and how we walked up the road?"

"Yes—and perhaps a bit more than that. But the Coroner doesn't mean to go very deep. He'd have allowed more time if he had. It'll be just evidence of the state he was in, and 'temporary insanity' in the routine way. It's how he means to deal with the adjourned inquest that's not so easy to tell. Coroner friendly to you?"

"Mr. Duckworth? Yes, of course. We've met often enough. I don't know him well. Rather fussy, but not a bad sort."

"I was thinking—if you should be recalled to the box—"

"Is it likely I shall?"

"I don't know. There are circumstances in which I might ask for you to be recalled myself. It's all a question of how it goes."

"You don't think there'll be more trouble now? They won't adjourn it again?"

"I can't say. I don't anticipate that. It'll be a walkover for us, more likely than not. But I just wanted to give you one tip. You ought to be quite clear as to whether the drawer was open or shut."

"Is it so important which?"

"Not at all. But it's important you should be sure."

Lady Denton looked at him with eyes that did not fall, though he thought he saw a slight pallor under her delicately painted skin. She said with a slow, challenging deliberation: "You think you know what happened when Daniel died?"

"Yes," he said, with equal deliberation, "I think I do."

"But you don't know how it happened—how it came to that, and why it couldn't be any other way."

"No," he acknowledged. "No one could. We may be thankful— we lawyers, I mean—that that is more than the law requires."

"And that is why no trial was ever fair."

He did not deny that. He had often thought that, while the leaving of certain classes of crime unprobed, and the criminals untraced or unpunished, might lead to greater evils, very difficult to assess; yet, in very numerous instances, far more human misery was caused, even more social harm occasioned, possibly even more injustice done, by the probing of such a tragedy than if its neighbours had glanced aside.

There was something to be said for the old primitive Saxon law by which the men of his own hundred—the men who knew him— would consider the circumstances under which their neighbour had committed an act of violence, and decide whether they would stand by him or cast him out. And there was surely a sounder equity in the custom by which, if it were decided that a monetary penalty would properly close the event, the fine went to the pocket of the injured man or his relatives, and not to the community, as it does today.

So he might think, in an idle mood, but what had such doubts to do with the present case? He might think he knew—or at least partly knew—what happened when Sir Daniel died, and he might have a theory of the events which had led thereto, but these did not necessarily justify the event. And as to what had happened since, he had no more than a puzzled doubt. He might be thankful again that the law, finding facts sufficiently difficult to ascertain, concerns itself with no more than the consequences of human action, even to the absurdity of the proposition that a man who shoots at another with intent to kill is held to be less guilty if he be unable to aim straight.

But if these thoughts, or the assimilated result of their previous digestion, were in the background of Mr. Wheeler's mind, they were not sufficiently dominant to distract his attention from the practical problems with which he was now concerned.

"I suppose nothing," he said, "is quite fair. That is the price we pay for the gamble of life, without which it might be too dull to endure. And if absolute justice could be obtained, I suppose some of us might hesitate as to whether it were exactly what we require."

"Yes," she said frankly, considering this with the little puzzled frown that her habit was at such times, "I think we might."

"And what we have to consider now is the verdict at which we should aim tomorrow."

"Need I consider that?"

"No, it is my business rather than yours. But I should like you to understand: when you gave evidence before, you expressed a belief that Sir Daniel had committed suicide, and I have heard you argue since in the same way. There are three possible verdicts that might be brought in tomorrow. It might be suicide, or murder by someone definitely stated, either living or dead, or by some person unknown. Apart from that (but it's not likely in this case), the jury might say that Sir Daniel died from a bullet wound, but that there was not sufficient evidence to show how it happened."

"You mean it might have been an accident?"

"I mean that a jury might say that there is not sufficient evidence to enable them to solve a puzzle, and leave it there. That, like the much more probable verdict of murder against some person unknown, would leave it for the police to continue their investigations. The probabilities are a verdict of suicide, or that he was murdered by Gerard, either of which would be likely to be the end of the matter."

"Or," she said steadily, "they may say that he was murdered by me."

"No. I don't think we need consider that now. Not unless the Coroner's got some surprise to spring on us, which I don't anticipate. They're far more likely to say that Gerard did it, and that he has pleaded guilty by ending his own life; or if they feel that this isn't quite sure, they'd never be unanimous in putting it aside to accuse you. It would be a doubt, at the worst, and then they'd agree on 'some person unknown,' and leave it for the police to carry on or drop it, as they may decide."

"You think that's what it may be?"

"No, I think a verdict against Gerard's far the more probable."

"But," she hesitated, frowning again, "I don't think we should try for that. Neither of us"—she looked straightly at the lawyer as she said this—"believes it was. It doesn't seem right."

"It's a bit late to think of that now."

"Yes, perhaps it is, but why not suicide, as I've always said?"

"Well, for one thing, it's likely to be a much more difficult verdict to get, even if the Coroner would support it, which might be too much to ask. And, for another, it means a loss of thirty thousand pounds in insurance money to the estate."

"I shouldn't alter for that."

"No," he said. "You're one to stick to your guns. But I think you must leave this to me. What we want before all is to get the enquiry closed. It's a position where we may have to let matters go on to their natural end."

"I am sure," she said, making no further protest, "you will do what is best. I don't think there's much you can't. Was it you that got Redwin to clear off as he did?"

"No. I have never met the man since he was turned out from here, or had any communication with him. It must have been someone else. It was a mere chance that your letter didn't reach me too late. I don't often go into the office on Saturday morning, but it just happened I did."

"Yes," she said in a smiling incredulity at the form his denial took. "I thought it must have reached you on Saturday. But I didn't know that the man had gone—not till Monday night—nor what mischief he might have been trying to do."

"I am afraid you must have had some needless anxiety. Most people would have kept themselves better informed. But it was the wiser way to remain aloof, and show no concern."

"Yes, so I thought. And I had enough worry from—well, on Monday, without thinking of him."

"I have no doubt you had," he agreed, and seemed about to add something further, when the telephone rang.

"I expect," she said, "this is for you. Would you mind?" At which he rose and went over to the instrument to take the call.

"Yes," she heard, "Mr. Wheeler speaking. Thanks. Yes, we've had that from Mr. Leadbeater. Yes, of course she'll be there. So shall I, needless to say. Same jury? So I thought. Much the best way. I want to catch the three-seven back, if I possibly can. Yes, so I thought. Thanks." He rang off.

He came back to the table very cheerfully. "It's the finale tomorrow," he said, "and the curtain's going to be rung down. We should not halloo till we're out of the wood, but I think we can see the light through the trees now."

"I shall be very glad," she said, "when it is." Which was not hard to believe. "You'll stay the night now you're here?"

But he said no to that. He was really busy, and must get back. He felt that he had done all that was needed here.

Adelaide Denton went to lie down when he had gone, after telling Pauline that she was not to be disturbed. She wanted a quiet hour to think over the ordeal—the final one, she supposed—that was before her tomorrow. She must be clear in her replies, and, above all, she must be ready so that she would not hesitate at the wrong time. So Mr. Wheeler had guessed—had guessed part of the truth, if not all.

She remembered how she had hesitated over that question about the drawer. It had puzzled her because she could not see what implications it might have, and was afraid lest she might give the wrong reply. She had not tried to remember whether it had been open or shut. (It had been shut, of course. She had known that. She had shut it herself.) She had tried to think what the point of the question might be, so that she could answer accordingly. And the whole point had been to see whether she would hesitate in that way. People would call her a criminal if they knew. She supposed Mr. Wheeler thought of her thus, though it seemed to make no difference to him. But that might be because he was professionally engaged.

It was strange how different the truth was from that which was represented in books. She had read of murderers—of Bill Sykes, of Eugene Aram, and others—and of the tortures of remorse and mental anguish that they endured, making them, even without the retribution of men, like pariahs among their kind. But she felt nothing of that. In fact, she felt much as she had done before all this trouble had occurred. Lonely, yes. Worried, yes. There were thoughts that would try to force themselves on her mind at times, which must be put down with a firm will. There were panics of sudden fear.

But she felt no fundamental change in herself. Nothing that would make it seem less monstrous that she should be put in gaol than it would have been if Daniel had been alive today. (And how furious he would have been at the thought that anyone bearing his name should be treated in such a manner!) It was being found out that had been her one fear from the first, and she had not feared that overmuch in her normal moods. At the very worst, it could never be really *proved*, and there would be thousands to take her side. But tomorrow would be the end of that ugly fear.

In the privacy of her locked room, she opened the little safe where her jewels lay, and took out a book. It had a lock, to which the key had been attached by a few inches of red tape when it was bought, as it still was. (That was so like Gerard's futility, to buy a book with a lock and leave the key dangling beside it.) She turned over the pages to read certain of the latest entries, and to consider what implications they would bear, if it should fall into other hands. Curiously enough, they were so worded that they would help her rather than not.

But to have let the diary be found would have been a needless and foolish risk all the same. It would lead to more questions, more talk, and talk is a dangerous thing. It is always hard to tell where it may lead, or what hidden pitfalls may be fatal to those who think it an open road. She had got it from Gerard's room the first night that he disappeared. She had gone over everything in the earliest daylight hours (not wishing that a light should be observed there during the night). She had not (she thought) been foolish enough to attempt its destruction. Books (she had read) are not easily burned completely.

If it were found (but how should it be, in her safe?), she would say that, of course, she had not destroyed it. Why should she, having nothing to fear? She had simply removed it, knowing that Gerard would not wish it to fall into strangers' hands. (Or, perhaps, in her anxiety to find what had happened to him, she had searched for its concluding entries, which had, in fact, been of no avail, except to show the distracted state of his mind.)

But when the inquest should be over, she would destroy it, burning it thoroughly, page by page. It would be morbid to get into a habit of taking it out and reading it when alone. (It did contain some very curious things. Things you would never have expected from Gerard.) But morbidity must be overcome. She would—perhaps she would—destroy the letters also, which it was really foolish, wildly foolish, to keep, as she had told Mr. Wheeler, in that half-admission, that she had already done. But to do that would need resolution of a much harder kind.

CHAPTER XXIX.

The Coroner, in the law's phrase, sat on the body of Gerard Denton, and the jury, who knew as much about the case as anyone else (except Lady Denton and, perhaps, Mr. Wheeler), before they entered the box, listened to the somewhat perfunctory evidence of how it was found, the injuries it had received, and the condition of the path from which it had fallen. They stirred to a quickened interest when Lady Adelaide Denton was called, and entered the witness box. She was quietly dressed, though not in black; for Sir Daniel, as was generally known, did not approve of that ugly convention, and had, indeed, expressly forbidden it in his will. She was rather pale but quite self-controlled, and looked as beautiful as she always did.

She was an important witness, being the last person, so far as was known, who had seen Gerard Denton alive, and having gone some distance with him on his fatal walk; but what she had to say could be soon told, and Mr. Duckworth, an elderly medical man, more at home with the injuries from which his subjects died than the legal and psychological questions which their exits raised, treated her gently, and with a disregard for the laws of evidence and the rules of examination which it is the high prerogative of all Coroners to exercise.

This method, joined to her own instinct of economy in untruth, gave her an easy passage, and supplied the jury with a vivid and accurate realization of the emotional atmosphere of the house from which Gerard Denton had gone out to die.

She had known, she said, that he had been asked to attend at the police station that evening.

"Did you know the purpose of that visit?" the Coroner asked.

"It was to make some alterations in a statement which he had signed previously."

"About Sir Daniel's death?"

"Yes."

"Did he appear alarmed at this prospect, or unwilling to face the ordeal?"

"He was a good deal upset." She added, after a second's pause, as though in explanation, or it might be in defence of the dead man: "Gerard got upset rather easily."

"Did he say or do anything to give you the idea that he might be intending to take his own life?"

"No," she said; and then, surprisingly: "And I don't believe that he was."

Mr. Duckworth looked puzzled as he took down this answer. He even began a word of protest, which got no further than: "But...," when she added: "I mean, he hadn't any such intention during the day."

"You mean he might have acted on a sudden impulse?"

She considered this. "It would be a more likely thing. If he ever made his mind up about anything, he always changed it in half an hour."

Mr. Wheeler, genuinely puzzled as to the events which had ended in Gerard Denton's death, and not at all sure that Lady Denton was telling all, or nearly all, that she knew, had a moment of admiration. "If it were deliberate acting," he thought, "it would be genius. She says she doesn't believe he intended suicide, and yet convinces the jury both of the sincerity of her own evidence, and of the impulsive instability which makes it plausible that he did." He saw that she was invincible because she was speaking truth, and truth is always the most potent weapon with which to sustain a lie.

But the Coroner was going on with his quietly leading, suggesting questions, taking her out on the final walk. "And this visit to the police station was still the sole topic of conversation?"

"Yes."

"And how far did you go with him?"

"Not very far. We stopped once or twice, and then went on when he started talking about it again. It may have been to the top of the hill. He said he couldn't stand any more hanging about the house. He'd walk on to Loudwater, and come back by the lower road in time for the interview at seven, and I said that was too far for me, and if I'd got to go back alone I wouldn't go any further. But I thought it might be the best thing he could do, in the mood he was in."

The examination was soon over after that, and it was not long before the Coroner was summing up, in a brief and rather perfunctory way, as one who went through a necessary preamble to reach a verdict already sure.

138

He explained shortly what the jury had to decide: the cause and manner of death. Beyond that they had no concern. There might be other matters concerning the dead man which he would have to ask them to consider later in another connection, but not now. Was it murder? There was no evidence to suggest it. There was no sign of a struggle. Was it accident? If so, what had led him of the road to that desolate and lonely spot? Was it suicide?

They had heard of the evident emotional stress under which he was labouring. There were people, even when absolutely innocent, who had a morbid horror of everything pertaining, however remotely, to the processes of the criminal law; and they had heard—he was not inviting them to go outside the proper scope of this enquiry—but they had heard that the accuracy of a statement which he made, in regard to a recent tragedy which must be in all their minds, had been seriously challenged, and he had been given an opportunity of altering his evidence, which he appeared to be fearful to do. It might seem that suicide—possibly on a sudden unpremeditated impulse—was very clearly indicated. But it was for them to decide.

The jury returned a verdict of "suicide while of unsound mind" without leaving the box.

It was then three minutes to twelve, and the adjourned inquest on Sir Daniel Denton was held immediately.

The Coroner, after a few preliminary remarks, including an injunction to the jury to put out of their minds anything that they had heard at the previous inquest, which it would be obviously impossible for them to do, promptly put Chief Inspector Pinkey into the box, from whom they heard an account of the bribery of the boy, and of the explanation, which might or might not be true, which Gerard Denton subsequently gave, including his admission that there had been angry words between himself and his brother at that last interview, which he had endeavoured to conceal.

He went on to say that, after these admissions, he had given him an interval of several days in which to consider what amended statement, if any, he would prefer to substitute for that which he had acknowledged to be untrue, and how, the second appointment not being kept, he had gone, in company with Superintendent Trackfield, to Bywater Grange, and there learnt from Lady Denton how he had left the house in the earlier evening. Briefly, but sufficiently, he narrated the later details of the finding of the body of the missing man, which had been given more fully at the previous inquest.

There was a moment's pause as Inspector Pinkey left the witness box, during which many eyes were turned upon Tommy, sitting apprehensively on a bench at the rear of the court, his usual cheerful grin effectually suspended as he waited to hear the summons which would oblige him to repeat his story—or, rather, one of his stories—in that strange and awful publicity.

But the Coroner and Inspector Pinkey had exchanged a few words on that subject already, and had agreed—the idea had been gently suggested by the Inspector—that he was an utterly unreliable witness, and that no useful purpose would now be served by putting on the records what might be no more than a varied lie. The Inspector had decided that it would be best to obtain such a verdict from the jury as would finally close the case, and the amended version of Tommy's narrative, if it should endure cross-examination unshaken, could only confuse the minds of the jurymen with a useless doubt.

Mr. Duckworth had agreed, though with some hesitation, that, so far as he was concerned, Tommy should not be called. The boy had supported Gerard Denton in an account, which they had subsequently admitted to be untrue, he having been paid to lie. He had then, from whatever motive, truly or not, supported an amended narrative which was alike in so far that it appeared to clear Gerard from suspicion of his brother's death. But when Gerard had been invited to embody this second account in a written statement, he had avoided the appointment, and it had become an officially recorded 7fact that he had preferred the desperate alternative of suicide. What reliance could now be placed on anything that the boy might say?

But Mr. Duckworth saw that a demand for his evidence to be taken might come from Mr. Wheeler, either in the interests of Lady Denton or of the reputation of the dead man, whom he had also legally represented, and, if such a demand were made, he did not feel that it could be refused. Now he looked interrogatively at Mr. Wheeler, who shook his head in reply. That astute gentleman saw that nothing could be gained by any evidence that Tommy would be likely to give, and some risks that he would be glad to avoid.

The disinclination to hear Tommy's further evidence was unanimous, unless among the jury themselves, who were not consulted, and too overawed by the solemnity of the tribunal to express any individual inclinations that they might feel. They soon found themselves listening to the Coroner's summing-up which he gave them in an easy, competent, conversational manner, with no more than an occasional reference to the notes of the previous hearing, and in such a way that, while he explained that the responsibility of the verdict was theirs, he made equally clear, as his custom was, what he expected that verdict to be, and he would have been surprised indeed if a jury of Beacon's Cross had been sufficiently disrespectful to disregard his wishes.

After commencing with a routine exposition of the law as it affected such cases, and of the various verdicts which it was within their discretion to render, he went briefly and clearly over the admitted facts of the case, and then came to the core of the problem which was before them.

"You have first to consider," he said, "whether the evidence is consistent with a theory of self-destruction. When you examine that possibility, you observe that it is not supported by any evidence of an affirmative character. No one has come forward to say that Sir Daniel had ever threatened to put an end to his life. Those who commit suicide often leave letters or other documentary evidences of their intention. There is no such document here. Those who take the desperate remedy of self-destruction are usually of unbalanced character, or suffering from acute mental disturbance, or the ravages of disease. There is no such condition suggested here. In fact, there is no discernible motive at all.

"It might be rash to conclude that, because no motive has been discovered, therefore none existed, either in fact or imagination, but where no motive can be discerned, and where no disposition to self-destruction has been observed, it is natural to look the more closely at the circumstances of the case before admitting the theory of suicide in explanation of the tragedy.

"As to that, you have heard the evidence of the position of the wound, and the course which the bullet took. You have heard the opinion of Sir Lionel Tipshift that it is not reasonable to suppose that such a wound should be self-inflicted."

Mr. Wheeler rose. "I have on my notes that he stated it was a possible thing."

The Coroner paused a moment to consider the implication of the interjection. He had not supposed that Mr. Wheeler would advocate the theory of suicide, and, had he intended to do so, he would have expected that he would have taken a different line at an earlier stage. He was right in that. Mr. Wheeler did not now propose to go far enough to risk the possibility that the jury's verdict might be one of *felo de se,* or suicide while of unsound mind.

He recognized, as a practical man, that he would almost certainly fail in the attempt, and it might be a real though probably not an insuperable obstacle to collecting the insurance money, for the company to be able to point to the fact that the family, through their solicitor, had publicly contended that Sir Daniel had taken his own life. But, feeling assured that there was no risk that the jury would bring in such a verdict, and facing the contingency—still possible, however improbable it might be—that the case would end with Lady

Denton in a criminal dock, he saw advantage in the fact that he would then be able to bring into prominence that admission that Sir Lionel had made, that suicide was a "possible" thing.

The Coroner looked for a moment at Mr. Wheeler's inscrutable face, and then at his notes of the evidence taken on the earlier day, and said dryly: "Yes—possible." But the tone did not matter. The word was there. Mr. Wheeler, well content, listened silently as the Coroner resumed:

"You will probably dismiss from your minds, for the reasons that I have stated, any theory of self-destruction, and so arrive at the real problem of by whose hand, and whether by accident or design, Sir Daniel Denton was killed. No theory of accidental death has been put forward, and the fact that the weapon must have been taken from his own drawer may seem to discount that possibility.

"You may also be able to eliminate any question of homicide other than deliberate murder when you consider, not only that the pistol must have been taken from the drawer, but that there was no sign of a struggle, and that the shot came from behind. You may also decide that it is at least a probable deduction that whoever knew where that weapon lay, who could secure it, either with Sir Daniel's consent or without his knowledge, and who could take up that position, immediately beside or behind him, in his own study, must have been known to him, and, most probably, a member of his own household.

"Examining every possibility, as you are bound to do, you may first consider the position of Lady Denton. Her own account is that she was in the drawing room, at the other side of the hall, when she heard the shot, and that she ran at once to her husband's side. When she found him a dying man, she screamed for help, as any woman would be likely to do. She says that when she reached the room the murderer had left, which is quite possible, the window being unbarred, if not actually standing open at the time. You may think that the murderer, whoever he was, would be unlikely to remain after the commission of such a crime, and that Lady Denton's account in this particular is no more than you would have expected to hear.

"Her tale, in itself, was simple and natural, and was not shaken in the course of her examination. Such witness is most often true.

"Then you will come to the position of Gerard Denton. I do not know how he may have impressed you in the witness box—I know how he impressed me—but as he gave his evidence, and as it was supported, as you will doubtless remember, by that of Lady Denton, and of the gardener's boy, he appeared to be removed from any suspicion of complicity in the crime.

"That evidence was in accordance with written statements which had already been taken by the police—very properly taken—before the inquest was held. Such evidence—apart from that of Lady Denton—and those statements we now know to be false. You have heard Inspector Pinkey, and you know the dreadful alternative which Gerard Denton preferred to the ordeal of explanation. You may find—but it is entirely for you to decide—that the conclusion is irresistible. But the decision is yours.

"Should you feel that, while you are satisfied that murder was committed, the evidence does not point to any person with sufficient certainty as the perpetrator of the crime, you may render your verdict in that way. But should you, as reasonable men, and on such evidence as you would regard as conclusive in the conduct of your own affairs, consider that the case is proved beyond serious doubt, you will, I feel sure, do your duty as citizens, and render your verdict without fear or favour, either toward the living or the dead."

Mr. Duckworth had omitted one or two things that he had meant to say, but he had led himself up to an impressive climax, as he usually did, and his dramatic instinct was sufficiently strong to cause him to cease at that point. He added briefly, on a lower note: "You will consider your verdict," on which there was a moment of whispering among the jury, and of bending over toward one another, so that it seemed that they might be about to agree without leaving the box. But, after that, the foreman exchanged an inaudible word with the usher, and they rose and filed out to the seclusion of the jury-room.

After they were gone, the usher had a whispered word with the Coroner's clerk, Mr. Leadbeater, who had another with the Coroner, who announced that the Court stood adjourned until the jury should be ready to render their verdict. He retired to his own room, and a stir of conversation arose among those who remained.

Lady Denton, sitting beside Mr. Wheeler, showed no outward sign of emotion, though she found it somewhat difficult to follow the anecdote which he considered appropriate for the occasion, and which he told with force and humour.

"It isn't worth getting up," he said at the first. "Ten minutes will be about their time." Other experienced observers took the same view. But as the minutes passed, and they did not return, he began the tale of an inquest he had attended three years before at which the jury had brought in a verdict so perverse and startling that the Coroner had refused to accept it, and had sent them back to resume their deliberations.

143

"Not," he added, "that there's any danger of that here. It's just between 'Gerard Denton' and 'some person unknown,' and not much doubt even between those."

Lady Denton understood that he was intending to allay any disproportioned anxiety she might be feeling, and to prepare her against the remote contingency that the jury might have an opinion of their own with which to surprise the Court.

It was half an hour later that the Coroner resumed his seat, and the jury filed back into the box.

The foreman stated in reply to the usual question, that they were agreed on their verdict. They found that Sir Daniel Denton had been murdered by Gerard Denton, who had committed suicide when he had seen that he could not otherwise escape the penalty of his crime.

The Coroner said: "Thank you, gentlemen. It is a verdict with which I entirely agree." And entered it in somewhat different phraseology. They came out of the jury box with a pleasant sense which his words had given them, that they had shown themselves to be somewhat cleverer than their fellow men.

Lady Denton rose, shook hands with Mr. Wheeler, giving him a word of thanks which he surely deserved, and passed out quickly to her waiting car. She went through a little crowd round the door, from which there arose a sympathetic murmur that almost grew to a cheer.

Inspector Pinkey said he would go back on the three-seven—the same train that Mr. Wheeler was taking. There would be just time for a late lunch at the Station Inn. Would Superintendent Trackfield join them? No, he thought not. The Superintendent was the one living man who had reason to be dissatisfied with the verdict they had just heard, which convicted him of an incompetence which he did not readily admit to his own mind. Perhaps it was natural that he was the one man also who was not entirely convinced that the verdict was soundly reached.

"I wish," he said, "that I could be more sure than I am that that boy isn't telling the truth."

Inspector Pinkey looked at him curiously. He asked: "Does it matter now?"

It was a question to which the Superintendent found no reply.

CHAPTER XXX.

Adelaide Denton lay in a moonlit room and looked up at the stars. She remembered—she had read somewhere—that if anyone tries to put a matter aside, refusing to think of it, it may remain festering in the mind like a sore that is surface-healed; but if it be boldly faced and considered, it will fade out in a natural manner. "There is nothing," she had read, "too terrible for a resolute mind to face it successfully; but it may be fatal to run away."

Well, she would face it. She would justify or condemn herself. She was not fond of running away.

Three weeks ago she would not have thought it possible that such things could enter her life. She had been unfaithful to her husband two years ago. But that was a dead thing. No one knew. No one suspected. No one ever had. And the man was dead. Even now she was not sorry for what she had done then. Not in the least. She had never had any mental difficulty in facing *that* sin. But she had been foolish, sentimentally foolish, to keep the letters. Foolish beyond words. She would admit that. But for that she would not have killed—*have had to kill*—two men.

Things might not have happened as they had if she had not detected Redwin's dishonesty and denounced him to her husband. "You'll be sorry for this before you're through." Those had been his words to her as he had left the house, and, after that, she had found that the letters were gone. She went over every incident in her mind, not seeing where she could have acted differently, till she came to the day when she had seen the postman drop the afternoon letters into the box.

She had been just too late—a mere five seconds too late—to take them from him. It had all hinged upon that. And among them had been the packet addressed to her husband in Redwin's unmistakable writing, the contents of which were so easy to guess, and which he must never see. She had seen the writing plainly through the small round glazed window in the letter box, which would have been too small, even had she broken it, for the packet to come through.

But she could have broken the box. She saw that now. In any way, with any tool, at any cost of fantastic explanation afterwards. But, instead of that....

Her mind went resolutely back to that time, two years ago, when she had gone with Daniel to Teignmouth, and after two days he had complained of so many things that she did not know which might be genuine, or whether all were mere excuses alike. It was depressing weather—a depressing place—the hotel cooking was putrid (he had always been particular about his food, which had made it so extremely silly when he had gone into the kitchen to quarrel with an excellent cook)—the telephone service was bad, so that he could not talk with his broker in London with certainty that his instructions would not be mistaken, as it was essential at the moment that he should be able to do. The last excuse—or reason—had been put forward as the decisive one. He would go back at once. She could stay alone, if she pleased. She did not know whether he had meant that permission to be taken seriously; whether he had said it in a merely perfunctory way, relying upon her declining, as a matter of course, to remain without him; or even whether he had secretly wished, for whatever reason, that he could return alone.

But in her irritation at what had seemed a perversity of ill-temper, such as he was always liable to exhibit, she had replied that she saw no reason to leave: they had taken the suite for a month, and for that time she would stay. He had stared and said no more than: "Then you understand that you'll have to stay without me?" and had left for the train an hour later, with the parting words: "I suppose you'll find your way home when you've found it a poor joke to sit sulking here."

But she had not sat sulking there, nor had she found it a poor joke. She had gone out on to the beach that afternoon and made George Mansell's acquaintance, she scarcely knew how—perhaps he could have told her something more about that—and discovered later, amazing coincidence as it had seemed then, that his room at the hotel was next door to her own suite. Let her face what she had gained, and decide whether the price might not, after all, have been no more than was fair, which she could not object that she had now to pay. It was a price that she could not have foreseen, and had she done so it might—it most surely would—have deterred her from what she did.

But she could not grumble at that. Vaguely, but sufficiently, all the time, she had known it to be a law of the traffic in which she dealt. Those who go outside the bounds of moral or human law must buy in a market which will not bargain, nor mark its goods in a plain way. They must take and use that which they seek to have, and the price will not be discovered till it must be paid at a later time. That was fair enough, for it was a market where no one was bound to deal.

What had she had? A week of friendship, of companionship, such as she had not known that the world held: a week of delirious excitement, of passionate abandonment of restraint, of deliberate forgetfulness of all that had gone before, or that must be faced on another day: a week of awakening to the fact that the dream was done—that George Mansell must leave, even before she would be due to return to her own home. There was no question of flight with him, no thought of divorce. He went on service where he could take no woman, even had he been married to her. And six months later there had been the news that he was lost, and was doubtless dead.

She had not been much concerned at the time with any ethical aspect of what she did. She was one of those rather numerous people in whom the moral sense is never very strongly developed, because their own instinctive standards of conduct conform so easily to the environment in which they live. Fundamentally, she had always been her own law.

When temptation came with sudden, undreamt-of strength, her power of resistance was of an untested weakness. It might be truer to say that she did not resist at all, nor was she conscious of any shame.

That was partly because she had done everything with that cool economy of falsehood which was most natural to her character, and which her reason advised. There had been few public indiscretions. There had been numerous excursions, mostly by rail, to quiet places, to which they journeyed, for the first part of the way at least, in separate compartments.

When she had gone to George's room in the night, as she often had, it had not been done in a furtive way, but as boldly as though the hotel were hers, quietly, reasonably reliant upon the presumption that no one would be about at the hour she chose—or, if they had, she would not have gone to his door. But it had been no more than three yards, and who was there to hear her steps on the thickly carpeted landing? But no one could ever have seen her look out of her door in the night as one in doubt or afraid, or slip furtively across, as some foolish women have been likely to do, for such actions could not be hers.

And there had been letters during the next six months, which had come openly, as she had said that they must, and that also had proved to be a discreet boldness—if they had not been kept, as they so foolishly were. For that was before the extent of Sir Daniel's business correspondence had caused him to have the large locked letter box fixed up, of which he would keep the key. At the time, the letters had always been brought to her, and she ordered their distribution throughout the house. But, in any event, the idea that Sir Daniel would open her letters, or even display an unmannerly curiosity as to their contents, was absurd. His disposition was not of that kind. His faults were contrary. He was more likely to disregard that which he should in courtesy have observed than to pry into her private affairs.

So it had been. Those were days to which she had looked back with a keen regret, with a secret pleasure as well as a secret grief, but without any thought of self-condemnation invading her mind. It was not that she had seen any justification for what she did. She simply had not thought of that side of it at all.

Now, seeing the fruit it had borne at last, it must be looked at in a new way. For her own peace, for the integrity of her own soul, she must ask herself, was there justification for what she had done then? Later, she would have to ask herself the same question regarding other things—worse things in the eyes of the law, and perhaps in themselves—that she had done since. But she would do all in an orderly way. She meant to explore too thoroughly to have to go over the same ground again.

And when she asked herself that question, she saw, in a fundamentally honest mind, that only one answer was possible. There had been no justification for what she did. It was not a question of human conventions, or human laws. By her own act of marriage, she had pledged herself to Sir Daniel, in a manner which she had understood at the time, and it was a contract that she had not kept. Many contracts are broken, of many kinds. Some are broken of necessity, for which there may be no blame. But she saw that there are only two ways by which a contract may be broken without dishonour— that of necessity or of mutual consent.

Had there been a common understanding between them—had they agreed to separate, or that each should do after his or her own device, it would have been an utterly different matter, and the answer to the question she asked herself might have been less simple to find. But if a liability be assumed, or a contract signed, it is not enough to say, when the day of reckoning arrives: "I have changed my mind," or "I would prefer to spend the sum in another way." There must be payment, or honourable bankruptcy of resource, and all else is fraud.

That she had done wrong was a fact that she had no sophistry to refute, and she attempted none to her own mind.

But the thing having been unchangeably done, in what or where had she gone wrong at a later time? She knew that there were those who would say that she should have confessed her fault—that she should have told her husband what she had done, be the consequences what they might. But that was something, be it right or wrong, that she was unable to see. It seemed to combine weakness and folly in about equal degrees. It could have done no good. It would have done harm.

It would have troubled Daniel, and whether or not he would have forgiven her (which it was not easy to think), it would have disturbed his life. She had wronged him when she had been unfaithful to the vows of loyalty that she had made; she would have wronged him more had she told him what she had done. A fact may increase in importance in direct proportion to the number of those to whom it is known. It may be nourished to larger life. She saw that one who has committed a secret wrong may, by the weakness of confession, augment the sin, and it is a poor and selfish pretext that it will bring relief to the sinner's mind, even if that result be reasonable to expect.

No, what was done was irrevocable. There could be nothing left better than to put it aside. But she faced the further fact that that was what she had failed—what she had not attempted to do. She had kept the letters, the mementoes of a past happiness, as of a past grief, that she would not willingly put aside; and every day that she had done that, she had continued to break her faith. She had sinned as continuously as though she had gone each night to her lover's bed.

It was strange that she had never seen this before; that she had given it no thought. It was somewhat late to regard it now, but it must be done. She got up and switched on the lights, drawing on a dressing gown, for the night was cold. She went to her jewel safe where—incredible folly—the letters still lay beside Gerard's diary, and took them out. She went on to the further room, and was content with the light of a dying fire.

Soon the room was alive with a wider light, as she took the letters one by one—there were seventeen in all, as she knew well, but now she did not count them, and she would have found a new cause for alarm in the fact that the number was less by one—and dropped them into the blaze, and as she did so she surprised herself with her own tears.

Resisting after a time a mood that was alien to her own normality, she watched the dry sheets burn till she was sure of the illegibility of the last blackened ash, and went back to her bed.

The destruction of the letters, and the eruption of feeling that the act had caused, had given her a sense of expiation which was at least a step to the peace she sought. It was an act that she might regret at tomorrow's dawn, but it was now as irrevocable as were those other episodes of adultery and murder, of which they were fruit and cause. Their destruction was an auto-suggestion that the whole could be put away, as though she had written *Finis* to an ended book.

CHAPTER XXXI.

Adelaide Denton went back to bed, but she did not attempt to reach the haven of sleep. She had faced the fact that the first cause of the incredible incidents of the last three weeks which had made her a widow, and stained her hands with the blood of those of her own house, was a sin for which she could find no defence by her own code. Nothing could alter that. Seeing it, she had done what she could (it seemed much to her) by the destruction of the letters, to regret and condemn it as a memory she could never be able to nourish again, as she I had done till a month ago.

Nothing could alter that. But, for her own peace, she had to face further and more sinister things.

She would still take them in the order in which they came, trying to separate her individual responsibility from the acts of others, and the impact of surrounding circumstance.

There was first her unintentional accusation—almost unintentional if not quite—against Redwin, which had had such incalculable consequences. That, at least, was a matter in which she could find no blame for herself. It was true that he was a man whom she had disliked to have in the house, and had distrusted utterly from the day he came. But Daniel had never, to her thinking, been very wise in the men with whom he associated. Having some ability of his own, though much less than his dignity required that those around should attribute to him, he was always disposed to the society of cleverer men who would be obsequious to himself. There was no doubt that Redwin, in his own way, was a clever man; and he had adopted just the right degree of deference at the first to establish his position on the footing for which he schemed.

It was true that she had always been willing to expose any error of conduct or manner which might not otherwise have come to Sir Daniel's notice, and this attitude had made it natural for the man to interpret her motive, in the incident which had led to his expulsion, in the most hostile way. But, even had that been as true as he had supposed, was it not fully justified by its result? Had she realized the full meaning of the letter which came by chance to her hands, and the extent to which the man was defrauding her husband, it was as much her duty as her obvious interest to lay his perfidy bare. On that point, she could be easily acquitted at the tribunal of her own mind.

Next to that—it seemed a venial fault when considered beside the consequences to which it led—she had been careless about her keys. More than once. Probably many times.

When Redwin had been ordered to leave the house, and had gone upstairs to pack, he must have entered her room, picked up the keys from her dressing table, opened the safe, taken the letters out— he had not been fool enough to touch the jewels—dropped them into his pocket, and walked out unsuspected and unobserved. It had been as simple as that.

At that time he could afford to be bold, having little left that could be lost in that house, but there must have been an earlier day when he had done the same thing; at least, so far that he must have taken her keys and examined the contents of the safe, or how else would he have known where to go, and what he would be able to take?

So her mind went on to the moment when he had gone with a muttered threat against herself, which she had met with a confident smile. But that confidence had fallen flatly enough when, on the next day, she had found that the letters were gone, and formed an instant guess of who held them then. So far, she could see no fault in herself, except that she had been careless about the keys.

Then the next day there had been the letter from Redwin, which had said so much—and implied so I much more. She remembered the first panic of fear, the fierce impulse of anger which had been so hard to subdue to the smiling casualness which the situation required; for she had opened the letter at the breakfast table, with Daniel at her side, and in an unusually genial mood, perhaps feeling the relief of Redwin's dismissal.

She had gone, when breakfast had been over, to the quietude of her own room to decide what she should do. She remembered how fiercely she had resolved that the letters should *never, never* come to Sir Daniel's knowledge, let the cost be what it might. It was hard to decide whether she had been right or wrong about that, or even what her strongest motive had been. It had not been wholly selfish, she knew. It was only fair to allow that. She was not a coward. She was not physically afraid of anything that Daniel could say or do. Neither was she financially dependent upon him. But she had seen, as the prospect of exposure became near and real, that, whether they should part in consequence, or remain together, the revelation would be likely to have a more disastrous effect upon Sir Daniel's happiness and peace than upon hers. His pride would suffer almost equally, whether he should decide to expose or conceal the wound. If they should part, it would be found by both that he had been far more dependent upon her than she on him, in a score of ways.

And if her resolve had not been entirely selfish, as between Daniel and herself, neither had it been dominated by her determination, fierce and obstinate as that also had been, that Redwin should not be the means that should put her to such a shame—that he should not triumph through her.

She had shown this when she had abased herself to attempt to pay the price which the blackmailer had asked, and had proposed to Daniel to take him back. But she had not been foolish enough to have intended that he should become an inmate of the house again with those letters in his possession, to be used as a lasting threat. She had thought to bargain with him at once on his return. Either he must hand them back then, or she would go herself to Sir Daniel and tell him all. Faced by that alternative, there would have been no doubt of what he would do. And after that he would have had to hold the position he had regained, if at all, by his own behaviour.

Should he tell of the incident at any future crisis, she had prepared the tale that they were her sister's letters, not hers, which she had afterwards used in half admission to Mr. Wheeler. With the letters no longer in Redwin's possession—with the assertion, true or not, that they had been destroyed—it would have been sufficient, as she supposed, to have borne her through. And she was probably right in that, for she had a life-long habit of truthfulness, which would have been her support, and which had been her friend in the deadly perils of the enquiry of the past week, inducing that economy of falsehood which gives the best prospect of life to a lonely lie. But the letters themselves, as she knew well, would have been fatal to such a tale.

Had she done wrong when she had asked Sir Daniel to take Redwin back? She could not see that she had. It had an aspect of cowardice which she had disliked, and which was unpleasant to think of now; but, joined as it had been to the resolution that the letters should be surrendered as its immediate price, it might have proved the best way—best for Sir Daniel, as for herself. There would have been no question of her being in the power of a man in the house who might have misused his position to betray her husband's interests for a second time.

153

But, having failed to secure his return, which was the point at which the crisis came, what should she have done differently, and to what issue, rather than to that which would, even then, had she considered the worst possibilities that might confront her, have seemed an incredible and monstrous end?

For it was only fair to recognize that. The moment it happened—even five seconds before—it had not been meant. The thought of murder had never entered her mind.

It was not that she had resisted temptation, or considered it and put it aside. The thought had not been there. It had not attempted intrusion, and, had it done so, it would not have been rejected with difficulty, nor considered as possible; it would have been recognized as utterly alien and absurd.

She saw, too, that in the crossing of the thousand complicated chances that surround our lives, it was no less than an enormous improbability that circumstances would have converged to the event—perhaps a million to one—even a few days before. Perhaps a million to one against the same precedent circumstances, so far as she was responsible for them, leading to such an end, if her life should be lived again to an equal point. Or was it fated, as some will hold, so that we do no more than weave our own infinitesimal part of a pattern designed before in the mind of God?

More confusing than that, if we would award praise or blame in a just scale, either to others or to ourselves, she went on to see that human actions, for good or evil, are not of a certain quality or a level worth. The individual will not always reach to the same circumstances in the same way. The scale may be turned by a feather's difference of health or mood, or of some precedent inconsequent thought or emotion, so that the occasion for noble conduct may be embraced or rejected, the temptation to baseness be accepted or put aside, with irrevocable consequences, and a future fundamentally changed by a moment's act—and the opposite possibilities were latent before in the one individual, to lead—if so they do—either to heaven or hell.

But it would lead her nowhere to speculate in such ways as these. Her mind went back capriciously to recall a moment when she had been a small child in a sunlit room in a primitive school in Wales. She had forgotten her own task to look at the weird signs of an algebraic problem which an older girl at the next desk had been set to solve. She remembered now how the bar of light that came through a half-drawn blind slanted across the desk. The signs meant nothing to her. The problem—simple enough, no doubt—was beyond any possibility of solution by her. And then, pleasant and clear in its admonition, there came the sound of Miss Milford's voice: "Adelaide, suppose you do the sum on your own slate."

That was what she had to do now. There might come a time when she would know how the universe is controlled, and to what end; but, as yet, with the human brain that she had, its symbols could mean nothing to her; its problems could not be solved. She must do the sum on her own slate.

Suppose she had gone to Redwin and bought him off? She had thought of that and rejected it with deliberation, though against the urgency of her natural fear. She had decided, deliberately, that he was not likely to fulfil his threat. She had heard, and her reason had supported the argument, that in all cases of attempted blackmail it is the first payment that is the fatal error. For the threat is impotent, if once it be executed. Redwin might send her husband the letters, but it was certain that he would not reinstate himself by such means. Only while he held them, and only if they could work on her fears, would they be useful to him.

But there had been another factor which had been potent to turn the scale, that of revenge. Yet she could not say that she had overlooked this. She had measured it deliberately against the self-revelation which it must imply, and what effect the man might expect it to have on Sir Daniel's mind. Redwin had been turned out of the house on the discovery of dishonesties which might still be the basis of a criminal charge. Would he risk so great a fall (she had not known, and did not guess now, how familiar his life had already been with the interiors of English gaols) as must result if Sir Daniel were stirred to a new anger toward the thief and revealer of those letters, so that he would have attacked him with every weapon the law supplied?

To everyone who knew Sir Daniel, both in passion and pride, it was a very probable thing, and the letters need not, indeed would not, have come into the picture at all. Sir Daniel might have turned her out, or given her the harder part of living as a wife who was very generously forgiven, and very secretly shamed. But in either event, he would not have been likely to let the man go free who had discovered and exposed the unsuspected stain on the honour of his own home. So she had decided that Redwin sought to frighten her with a threat that he dare not use.

Well, she had been wrong. But it was an error of judgment. It was no worse than that. She could not even call it a foolish error. She thought, on the same premises, she would decide again in the same way. And she might have been right this time. Who knew on what quickly regretted impulse, in what abnormal mood, the man might have dropped the packet into the post box? How quickly he might have regretted the action which he would have been powerless to undo? No, she could not blame herself, even for folly that, when her effort to get Daniel to reinstate him had failed, she had decided to do no more.

But she had not been careless. She had watched the posts. On two occasions she had made pretexts to get the key from her husband and clear the box herself. On the second she had kept it until he had asked for it at a time when it was beside her hand, and she could make no pretext to keep it back. Twice she had met the postman, so that he had given the letters to her. And (of course, as she told herself), there had been no occasion for alarm. She had vexed herself—had degraded herself—for no cause. Probably that might be the extent, she had thought, of Redwin's calculated revenge. To cause her to watch the post; to live in continual dread. If he had sufficient imagination, he might see his revenge complete, even though he should toss the letters on to the fire and give them no further thought.

And when she had thought this, and seen that she danced to the string he pulled, even while he did nothing at all, her hatred of him flamed as fiercely as when she had first thought of his reading those letters; those secret, private lines. If she had ever had murder in her heart, which she did not think, or if there were anyone that the world held she could murder now, or any circumstances in which she could contemplate such a crime, it would be Redwin whom she would have no remorse to destroy.

Any circumstances in which she could contemplate such a crime? Circumstances had arisen already in which she had not merely contemplated—or, rather, without contemplating—she had killed two men. Yet the thought had been genuine; it seemed natural still. Was it that she was not a murderess by instinct? Was she not different from her kind, from a million others who had not been tried in the same way? Or who would have come through differently, not from any nobler qualities, but because they were inferior in courage, in resolution, in clear-sighted recognition of consequences, to that which she might happen to be?

It was a fact, at least, that she was not conscious of any change, any degradation, even of any depth of iniquity in herself, since she had done those deeds—those crimes as the law would say—these sins as she did not doubt that they were. Was it that no one did? Or that human retributions were the controlling dread? Or, more probably, that character and circumstance varied in such myriad ways that no two cases could be alike in a million years?

156

She felt no change in herself—but only that she must face the facts, must measure what she had done, must understand all it was, all it implied, and decide how, and how far she could put it by. And the letters were ashes now.

Her mind, delaying to face the central facts which it had so nearly approached, wandered back into Dorset woods, and heard the voice of a dead man praising her hair, as Daniel had never done. And so she came through the ended familiar grief to the comfort of sleep.

CHAPTER XXXII.

She waked to the sounds of Pauline's light movements beside the bed, and of sugar falling into the cup. She was aware at first of a vague sense of sorrow and loss, for which she could remember no cause till recollection returned to her wakening mind. Then the sight of a firelit room sinking to darkness, as the ashes of burnt paper blackened within the grate, came back to her mind, and a desolation therewith that was not lessened, though it may not have increased, with fuller realization of all the sombre happenings of the last three weeks.

But the mood of introspection had passed; and grief and memory were put firmly aside as the practical question arose of whether the last scrap of paper had been consumed, or would be liable to be read by Pauline's loyal but intelligent eyes. She had an impulse to say that Mabel had better do the grate in her room this morning, knowing that, even if she could read them, any still legible words would be of no meaning to her incurious eyes. But the habit of courage and common sense altered her words to: "I shan't need the fire in my own room much before lunch, so you'd better do upstairs first. I'm going into the garden to see Bulger, after I've finished with Cook this morning."

Pauline said, "Yes madam," in her deferential routine way and went out. Lady Denton did not propose to risk being seen raking over the ashes, but she resolved that she would be back in her own room before Pauline would reach the task of clearing the grate. It would be done under her own eye, and she would be able to make some casual remark about the mess she had caused by the burning of papers she had been sorting out, so that it would be evident that it was not a matter to which any secrecy was attached.

As to Bulger, she had told him yesterday that she would be coming out this morning to decide the fate of certain poultry of advancing age, and delinquent fruit trees which he wished to destroy, but which she was anxious to save, and she knew the battle would not be easy to win. There were times when Mr. Bulger was very deaf.

Mr. Bulger's brother-in-law kept a poultry farm on the High-combe road, and held a strong opinion, which had Mr. Bulger's steady support, that the fowl pens of Bywater Grange required a fresh supply of laying pullets in the autumn of each year, for which those birds that occupied the pens already must be ruthlessly sacrificed. It was a question that usually had to be faced at a somewhat earlier date, but the occurrences of the last three weeks had caused even Bulger to recognize the expediency of deferring it until his mistress could give sufficient attention to what they both knew would be a strenuous conflict.

Had he had his own way, there would not be a bird at any autumn left alive for a second year. Had she had hers, there would have been little, if any, change in the pens, beyond the replacements required by accidental or natural deaths. As it was, she knew that there would be drastic weeding-out, and an order for Mr. Bulger's relative of at least half what he would have liked it to be.

Yet she had her own way in part, for there were birds which had won her favour by beauty of appearance, or conspicuous feats of laying, which had been there for five years, if not more, and which annoyed Mr. Bulger, as they would have annoyed the loyal brother-in-law of any poultry farmer, by declining to exhibit signs of senile decay, or noticeable falling off in the quantity of the eggs they laid.

Lady Denton grew fond of the birds that it was her custom to feed in the summer evenings when Mr. Bulger's departure took place at too early an hour, but she did not use an argument which would have been foolish in the gardener's ears. She answered his stout assertions that only pullets could be relied upon to lay in the winter months with the practical objection that, even if it were partly true, the extra eggs which the change would bring would be far less in value than the cheque which Highcombe Poultry Farm would receive; and with the still more indisputable fact that pullets lay smaller eggs than those which come from mature fowl.

She had an argument this morning of the usual length, leading to the usual compromise. There was a further skirmish respecting the destruction of an aged pear tree, from which she finally withdrew with little hope that Mr. Bulger had consented to hear her instructions. For, as there was no question in regard to the tree of a cheque having to be signed by her, he felt freer to exercise the full prerogative of his deafness in that direction.

She forgot, for the time, in the interest of this annual conflict, both the major shadows that vexed her mind, and her intention of being in her own room when the grate was cleared. But she returned in time to see Pauline commencing the task; and Mr. Bulger proceeded to the prompt irrevocable slaughter of as many hens as his conscience would allow him to misunderstand that Lady Denton had permitted him to destroy. "The Lord," he said, in substantially accurate quotation, "giveth us dominion over them," which the victims might not have considered disputable had they understood it, with all the theological implications attached thereto.

They went to their appointed end, which was that of being sold to a local poulterer for a fifth of the sum which the new pullets would cost. And Lady Denton, hearing the distant squawking of individual protest, which went on for some time as the gardener caught and slew them, was led to wish that the world were made in a better way. And, thinking this, she was led to another thought which might have shocked Mr. Bulger more even than if he had known how Gerard Denton descended the quarryside (though he would have been greatly surprised by that), for she considered that she would not like to be God, on whom the ultimate responsibility must surely rest, for every act of cruelty, every misery of man or beast, that the earth has known, if He have the power to stay it, and remains still. She was even led to wonder whether we pay Him a compliment when we postulate His omnipotence, and whether we could not render an easier loyalty if we supposed Him to be first, and yet finite in power, as she had been in her skirmish with Mr. Bulger on behalf of the hens that were dying now.

Then her mind startled itself with the incongruity of the idea that she, the treacherous murderer of two of the inmates of her own home, even of the husband that she had married and once thought she loved, should be vexed by such thoughts as these. She thought again, as she had done in the night, that she must resolve, for her own peace, what she was, and what she had really done, lest this shadow should darken and bear her down. And if it should continue restlessly beneath the surface of all she thought, as it did now, there would be a real continual risk that she would say some time, with the frankness which was her natural mood, perhaps at dinner among her friends: "But it's strange that I should feel like that," or "You oughtn't to ask me that, when you remember how I killed Daniel and Gerard."

She was getting to hate the dining table, where she now had her meals alone, and had been accustomed to having one of them on either hand. There had been an evening when she had genuinely forgotten, and sat a moment waiting for them to enter, in the normal way. She supposed that her mind was so wearied with continual thoughts on these subjects that it tried to put recollection aside. Even as she paused thus, it seemed that it made a conscious effort again, as though reality itself could be thrust away. It was too monstrous for belief. Surely she would wake from an evil dream.

"Pauline," she said, "I won't lunch in the dining room. You can bring me a tray here. And after that I'll lie down, and I shan't want to be disturbed. Not by anyone."

She was aware that she had almost added, "Unless the police come," although she supposed that that nightmare had left the house.

Certainly she must face a mood which must be destroyed, lest it destroy her in the end.

CHAPTER XXXIII.

The cook had called to her as she left the kitchen, "If you please, ma'am," and she had turned back for a moment, and said that she would telephone Porson to send the suet before ten in the morning—it had all turned upon that, at the last. If the cook had not spoken, or she had ignored her call, she would have intercepted the postman, and Redwin's letter would have come to her own hand. Had it done so, it is certain that it would have gone no further. She had been alone in the hall, and the letter had been so obvious in its bulk, and the undisguised handwriting of its address, that she had guessed what it was, even as she had seen it thrust through the letter box flap (for the door had been standing wide, as she would often have it on sunny days, being one who loved light and air, and was ill-content with a dusky hall). She could have stayed it, even then, with an undignified haste, or a quick word. It was too late to regret that now. So it had been. Blind chance, or settled destiny, or the malice of some spirit of evil, had tipped the scale to that end. The handwriting had been clear through the little disc of glass which enabled anyone to see whether the box were empty or not.

From that point, every word, every movement, almost every thought, was clear in memory, as though photographed indelibly on her mind. She had known that the moment for decision was short, for the postman must have passed in front of the study window as he came up the drive, and Daniel (who was there) would almost certainly have seen or heard him, in which case he would be likely to come out almost at once. And the mood that he was in—that he had been in for the whole day—could not have been worse for the reception of such a packet. Indeed, there had been few happy natural words between them since the quarrel about the cook. She was not exactly afraid of what would follow if he learned of her infidelity in such a manner, but she was resolved that it should not be.

The sudden realization that she had been too confident, too contemptuous, in dismissing the possibility that Redwin would fulfil his

162

threat, and that it was that spirit of overconfidence which had led her to an inadequate watchfulness, produced a resolution, both fierce and cold, that he should not shame her, should not succeed. The letters, by whatever means, should be kept from Sir Daniel's hands.

She had looked at the little disc of glass and would have smashed it instantly and drawn out the packet, leaving it to the future to find excuse, had she not seen that it was too large to come through the hole. She would not risk the ignominy of being found by her husband vainly trying to pull it out, for him to understand at last what she had been attempting to do.

As she hesitated, she had heard the opening of the study door and had turned away. She had passed him in the hall, and gone into the study herself, as he stooped to unlock the box. He would not stop to open, or even to look at the letters in the hall. She was sure of that, knowing his ways.

Memory came so vividly that, as she lay on the couch in the darkened room, she lived those moments again as actually, as inevitably, as they had first been.

It was in a folly of desperation, as she looked round the study while she waited to face him there, and to demand the absurdity that his own letter—and one in a hand he knew—should be handed unopened to her, that her eyes fell on the drawer where the pistol lay. She had time for decision, but not for thought. Quickly, resolutely, she reached the drawer, took out the pistol, and—of course—closed it again. (She should not—not have hesitated about that. It showed how delicately a lie must be nursed, if it is to live.)

She stepped back to the side table, which was against the wall facing the window, with the door on her left hand, so that when Sir Daniel stood at his desk he would have his back to her. She laid the weapon down among papers and books. She did not exactly hide it, but it lay so that it would not be seen without a near look. She had no thought to use it, except as a threat, and then only in last resort if all else should fail. She meant to use the fiction of her sister's letters before that, to induce him to give her the packet without looking at its contents.

He came in with the letters in his hand and his eyes on them. He walked to his desk without noticing that she was there. He stood looking through them, and laid two down, they doubtless being addressed to other members of the household. Perhaps he would give his first attention to others, letting Redwin's lie for a time where she could come forward and pick it up. She could talk with more assurance of success if it were in her own hands. But he did not do this.

He laid others down, keeping the bulkier packet in his hand. It was evidently that which engaged his curiosity first.

She came forward then. "Daniel, don't open that, please."

She was not normally deficient in self-control, and she made her voice as casual as she could, and spoke with as much of the confident familiarity which there should be between husband and wife as she could contrive to feign, their recent relations having been what they were. Had Daniel been different to her during the last week, it would have been a so much easier thing! It might even have seemed more nearly possible to have faced the truth. (But he could not guess that his temper would cost his life.)

Control her voice as she might, he must have heard the tension with which she spoke. He turned round, the unopened letter in his hand. He stared at her in an irritated surprise.

"I did not know you were there. What on earth is the matter now? Do you mean this? It's from Redwin Not open it? Why?"

"Daniel, if you'd listen to me a moment."

"Do I appear deaf?"

"I mean, I want to explain. There are some letters in there that are mine—I mean that Freda left them with me to keep for her."

"How do you know that?"

"He stole them from me when he left."

"And he's sending them back now? How have you made him do that?"

"He's not—I mean he's doing it in the hope of making trouble between us."

It was not the wisest thing to have said, or the clearest explanation to have made. His words, and still more his manner, irritable and half incredulous, drew her to foolish words, as they often would when they contended for lighter stakes. A puzzled suspicion came into his eyes as he answered: "You mean he's sending them to me—whatever they are—not to you? I think I'd better see what there is here, and we can discuss it better when we both know."

He tore the envelope open as he spoke, turning away from her.

"Daniel," she said, "please. They are private letters that Freda had from John."

"Well," he said, "what's the fuss if they are?"

She saw that he was drawing them out, and a sudden realization came that she had made it worse than it might have been by a useless lie. In another moment he would know that they were not what she had said. And with this thought there came a passionate determination that, even though she might tell him what they were, even though it might break them apart from that hour, the sacred, foolish words of a dead love should not come to be read by his contemptuous eyes. She picked up the pistol, and advanced toward him, divided between thoughts of threat, appeal, and belated confession, but resolved that he should first lay the packet down, at whatever cost. And then, though she stood at his back, she looked into his eyes.

Reflected clearly in the glass of the half-opened window, against the dark shadow of the rhododendrons, their glances met. She had not known—could not do more than guess, even now—whether he had seen what her hand held. But suspicion changed to accusation, and accusation to certainty, and certainty to a contemptuous condemnation in his eyes, in a moment's space. He might not guess what the letters were, but he knew she lied, and she knew that, in that certainty, there was not the faintest hope that he would resign the packet to her till he had probed what it might reveal. She did not consciously shoot. She would always be sure of that. Certainly she did not aim with intent to kill. But her hand tightened in an involuntarily physical response to the fierce resolution that those letters should not be read. And as he drew them out the deafening explosion filled the room, and in the same second he had collapsed, between her and the desk, like an emptied sack.

Up to that point her memory was so clear and exact that she had lived through the scene again as she had gone over it in her mind. But whether it called her murderess she could not be sure. Had she aimed with intent to kill, she felt that she must have done something better than that clumsy upward shot. Yet why was such a weapon within her grasp? Why had she taken it first? To threaten only? Then what of those stubborn resolutions that he should never read what the packet held? That Redwin should never boast that he had brought her to public shame?

Even for herself it was hard to say, and how—had she been accused—could a jury have judged more surely than she, when they would know so little of motive and impulse, and must guess the facts that were known to her? Well, it would not come to that now, and that certainty (as it seemed) had made it imperative that she should be cleared or condemned in the tribunal of her own mind. She saw at last that, to the point of the fatal shot, it might have happened a dozen times, in a dozen ways, that would not have ended thus. But there was little comfort in that, which is always true. The game of life must be played with no rehearsals at all.

After the shot, try as quietly, as persistently as she might, her memory was less clear, and perhaps the fact that it had had that effect upon her might be held to show that it was less than a purposed thing. She had screamed for help. That had been natural. There had been no acting in that. But she did not know now whether she had secured the letters then, or after Gerard went out, and before the palpitating cook came into the room. Nor was she sure when she had laid the pistol on the table, after she had first dropped it on the floor when it went of.

She remembered thinking that her finger marks ought to be wiped away—she thought that was after Gerard had come in, and she had said that whoever had shot Daniel must have left by the window, and he had gone out to look round the lawn. She could not remember wiping it, nor with what it had been done, but she supposed she had, or there would have been evidence against her which would not have been overlooked.

She saw, looking back, that it was queer that Gerard should have gone out so readily to look round, unless, indeed, he were relying on the probability that a murderer would not linger at the scene of his crime. He was not of a courageous reputation. But she knew now that he had left that window himself only two minutes before she entered. She had heard his voice in dispute with Sir Daniel as she had gone into the kitchen, and he must only just have left and entered the study as she came back to see the postman at the door. He had not gone out in bold pursuit of some strange shedder of human blood, but to ask Tommy whether anyone had entered by the study window, after he came out, or had left before his present appearance.

When he had come back with a half-frightened, half-curious Tommy, and the more phlegmatic Bulger behind him, and they had lifted a dead or dying man on to the couch, he had looked at her with eyes that were more scared than before. And when they were alone together a few minutes later, in that brief interval between the police (summoned on the telephone by her own instructions, and Pauline's frightened voice) had appeared, he had looked at her in the same puzzled, terrified way, and had said: "I can't make it out. I can't see who it could be. I was with him two minutes before." And then, as she only answered, her coolness returning before the panic he showed and the danger signal his words supplied: "It must have been very quick," he had added, with visibly trembling lips, "They'll think it was you or me."

"Well," she had said firmly, "we shall say it wasn't, and we should know better than they. We were here and they weren't."

"I hadn't left him two minutes," he had said again, in a helpless way.

"It must have been more than you thought."

166

"And Tommy says nobody went out."

"*Tommy*! You surely don't take anything he says seriously; he may have been looking up at the clouds."

He had said nothing to that, but gone out to the garden again, and when Superintendent Trackfield questioned the boy half an hour later, he had a pound note in his pocket and an urgent instruction to say that he had not seen Mr. Gerard come out of the window on the first occasion.

As the Superintendent's questions had, very naturally, been directed more particularly to ascertaining whether he had seen anyone come out after the shot had been fired, or go in before, Tommy had sustained this examination quite easily. And it was only next morning, when Gerard had told her what he had done, that she had given him reason to doubt the wisdom of such a bribe.

After that she had held her ground, lying no more than she must. She had resolved, with a clear wisdom, to speak and act just as she would have done if her tale had been really true—if, in fact, she had run into the room at the sound of the shot, to find her husband dead on the floor. By this means she not only took the course best calculated to impress others with her own sincerity, and the truth of the tale she told, but it had even begun to assume an illusion of reality to her own mind.

She was not sure that she could not have rested mentally content with that artificial memory, nor that it might not have gradually blurred the event itself, if the trouble had ended there. Even now, as she faced it with determination to put nothing aside, to condone nothing that she had done, she saw it as a tragedy in the Greek sense, in which evil comes from the hands of surrounding fates, rather than as the logical consequence of human action, or retribution for human sin. It was at least half true that it was a thing that she had not meant, and perhaps better than that. But the trouble had not ended there. There was the death of Gerard Denton to face, and that might prove to be the more difficult thing. Well, at least she would not be a coward. She would face what she had done, and the cause she had.

CHAPTER XXXIV.

It had been deliberately done. She must not disguise that. But the provocation, as it seemed to her—it might almost be called the necessity—had been very great. As they had talked on the High-combe road, she had seen, with that unflinching clarity of mind that would not avoid the logic of facts, however sinister they might be, that they were approaching a point when it would be Gerard or she who must face a criminal trial, with its almost certain consequence of conviction and penal misery, or a shameful death. And it would be Gerard's fault and not hers. The fact that it was her hand by whom Sir Daniel had died was incidental, not being the immediate cause of the danger to which she came. She was outfacing that. But Gerard's weakness and folly were drawing her back to the edge of the hateful pit.

For his cry was the same as it had been in the earlier day, but had become more insistent now. Women were seldom hanged. It would be fifteen years for her at the worst, and perhaps less. Fifteen years! In a gaol! She said no to that. She said that if he told the truth (in a frugal way), she would ask no more, and he would have no cause for the cowardly panic in which he shook. But he could not be relied on, even for that. He was full of fears that he would not be believed. That Tommy would have been persuaded to lie. That he would be detained at the police station, and never escape alive from the cruel blundering hands of the law.

She had not disguised from herself that there was a risk of that. And thence a risk for herself.

It was not only that Gerard, being so cornered, and thinking only of how best he could save his own neck from the rope, might be sufficiently circumstantial in details known only to themselves to obtain credence which would turn suspicion upon herself to an over-whelming degree. It was that, paradoxically enough, in the light of that which she was about to do, she knew that she could not let him stand in such a peril, and not come forward with the truth that would set him free. Hating and despising him as she did it, and cursing his cowardice as the cause, she yet knew that that was what she would do.

She had been afraid to turn back, leaving him in the mood he was, and afraid of the way he talked on the public road. An old woman had passed them with a curious look, overhearing something that he had said in too loud a voice. It is in such ways that gossip starts.

It had been with no other purpose than to draw him to a quieter path, while she made a last effort to stir within him a manhood that was not there, that she had proposed that they should turn to the quarry path. A path where it was thousands to one that no one would be at that chilly hour, which was yet too early for it to be the resort of wandering lovers from Beacon's Cross.

"Come this way," she had said, "we can talk quietly here." Honestly, she could not say when the thought of release had come; but it had been deliberately in her mind while she had continued further than he would have gone, where the path narrowed along the sheer edge of the pit.

And at last he had made it an easy thing. He had, naturally, walked on the outer side. There was not much room for two, walking abreast, unless one should be content to be torn on the brambled hedge. And as he talked in his agitation he had not been careful of where he went.

That was true, but she would not fool herself about that. At the last, it had been deliberately done. She remembered the thought that it must not be so that he could catch at her to save himself, so that she might be dragged to the same death. And then it had proved to be such an easy thing! She need not have pushed nearly so hard as she did. He would have overbalanced at a mere touch, and in ten seconds he must have died.

It had been far, far the best thing—might you not call it the only way?

No, not that, not the only way. Not, perhaps, the one most to her honour at this tribunal of her own mind, which she would not shirk. How much could be fairly said? It had been—paradoxically again she found some comfort in this—what Sir Daniel would have wished her to do. She was quite sure about that. He would have thought it better a thousand times that Gerard should come to a futile end than that the whole scandal should be exposed, and his wife degraded to a felon's cell and a felon's doom. Let it be settled amongst themselves. That was how he would have preferred it to be.

Thinking thus she saw that, had it been left to them, there would have been no cause for a second death. It was the interference of their fellow men, who would not be content unless they should know how Sir Daniel died. She must not turn aside to consider the ethics of that. It was her own conduct, her own guilt, that concerned her now.

And the fact was that she had pushed a man to his death, to escape the risk of social ruin, of shame, of possible death, and of the degradations of prison life which are worse than any possible death could be. She had done that in no moment of panic, in no mood of weakness to be repented in stronger hours, but deliberately, in the extremity of her own fear. And she would do it again. If she were to be honest with her own soul, she must recognize that. Given the same extremity of danger—through the weakness, or folly, or possible treachery of a man of Gerard Denton's type—she would do it again. She had no doubt about that. Yet, if he had been in peril of being hanged for her deed, she would have spoken the truth to save him, at whatever cost to herself. She recognized that, seeing just how base she was, and no more. And having faced these things, from the first pleasure of sin to the last (if last it were) of the bitter fruit that it bore, what should she do now?

She knew that there were some who would say that it was her duty now to confess and expiate her sin, handing herself over to the retribution that would be dealt out by her fellow men, but what use would there be in that? It would do evil to herself, wrecking her life. But was there any living man or woman or child to whom it would do the slightest conceivable good? It would bring peace, they would say, to her own soul. But even if that were true, and that such peace could be reached in no better way, which were two propositions of some apparent improbability, it would still be no more than a higher selfishness which would regard that as a decisive argument.

Apart from that, it might be said that it would complete Redwin's revenge. And, when she looked at the events of the last three weeks in a broader way than that of her own personal part therein, she saw that it was by his act, if not by his hand, that her husband and her husband's brother had come to their violent ends. That was the fruit that Redwin's revenge, really aimed at herself, had already borne. She could confess that they had died by her acts, and so make that revenge complete. He would read of it and be glad. (She did not know that he now had his own troubles, which would limit his opportunities of learning the news of the day.) That would be the one certain consequence, if she should make confession of the blood that was on her hands. She would complete Redwin's revenge. And the house would be broken up, the servants discharged.

She saw it in her imagination, desolate and empty, and the garden neglected and overgrown. She could see no result beyond that. Would it not be a nobler, as well as a saner thing, to put the past out of her thoughts and serve the present as best she could, reconstructing her life to some better purpose, both for herself and others, than it would be likely to serve in a prison cell?

Resolving thus, she got up. She had told Pauline not to disturb her till she should ring for tea. Now she touched the bell. She had done with introspection and vain regrets. *"The moving finger writes, and having writ...."* No one can alter the past. She must concern herself with that which would be written tomorrow; with that which was being written today.

Pauline came in with the tea. There was a letter upon the tray, and it was addressed to her in George Mansell's hand—the hand of the man who had passed into the desert silence two years ago, and since been reported dead.

She saw all that it meant—that it must mean—before she tore it open with a hand that trembled as it had not done for any stress of the past weeks. For she read the verdict of Heaven that she was to be punished, beyond the customs or imaginations of men, with the burden of a great joy.

CHAPTER XXXV.

Chief Inspector Pinkey saw the Assistant Commissioner. He laid two letters before him.

"These," he said, "were among Forsyth's papers at the room where he was caught."

Sir Arthur Renfrew read them.

"I suppose," he said, "you connect them with the Denton case?"

"Yes, and with the hints he gave that we were not on the right track."

Sir Arthur was silent for some time, recalling the circumstances of the case as they had been reported to him, in a very clear and logical mind.

"They raise questions," he said.

"Yes, several."

"Remotely, they give a motive for suicide."

"It wasn't that."

"No, I suppose not."

"I never have felt quite satisfied."

"You mean that the local police may have been right after all?"

"Yes. I don't know what conclusion I might have come to at last. Gerard Denton's suicide really took it out of our hands."

"There are the verdicts of the Coroner's juries. But when new evidence comes to our hands."

"Yes, but how far does it go, at the most? We might possibly work up a case. We might get a committal. A conviction wouldn't be easy."

"You think it's a case where we should let sleeping dogs lie?"

"We don't want to head for trouble we needn't have. And I'm a long way from being sure now, let alone seeing a case that could be legally proved."

"What sort of a woman is she?"

"Cool. Attractive. Got brains."

"The cold-blooded sort, I suppose? The type that we usually meet in this class of crime?"

"Not exactly. Not cold-blooded, I should say. Self-control, yes."

"Is she a type that might do the same thing again?"

"Normally, no. Presuming she did it once—I should say not."

Sir Arthur was a conscientious man, to whom expediency was not the sole god of the official mind. If he thought it right to reopen the case, he might not be deterred by the fact that it would be difficult, and possibly troublesome, with risks to the prestige of his office, if it should go wrong, all of which could be avoided by letting it lie quiet. He had imagination also that would look at times to the consequences of official acts, which were not always pleasant considerations. He said: "I won't decide now. You can leave the letters with me. Ask me about it tomorrow."

When Inspector Pinkey had left, he read the letters with care, considering what they revealed, both of their writers and those to whom they were addressed, and also what their evidential value might be.

One, which had been retained by Redwin when he had sent the packet containing the others to Sir Daniel, was from George to Adelaide. A love-letter with an old date. The other was from Adelaide Denton to "Mr. Redwin," written a few days before her husband's murder. Its phrases were carefully ambiguous, but, in the light of the other letter, and the fact that they had been pinned together as being parts of one matter, the meaning was not beyond reading by Sir Arthur's experienced eyes.

"Blackmail," he said to himself, "but beyond that...." It was a long way from convicting Adelaide Denton of her husband's murder. And to do that, Gerard Denton's part in the matter must be defined or cleared out of the way. And there was the verdict of the Coroner's jury. Even if it were wrong, of which there was no proof, it was hard to say how or by whose hand he had died, if it had not been his own. And there was no case of a miscarriage of justice having occurred from which the living might suffer now. The verdicts had applied only to those who were dead. And the case which must be reopened, if at all, to such dubious ends had been closed in an officially satisfactory way.

"No," he said at length, "I don't see that we can do anything more. I think we must let it be."

ABOUT THE AUTHOR

SYDNEY FOWLER WRIGHT (1874-1965) penned over seventy volumes of science fiction, fantasy, classic mysteries, historical novels, poetry, and non-fiction, many of them being published by the Borgo Press Imprint of Wildside Press.